Arthur C. Clarke's
Early Short Stories

Arthur C. Clarke's Early Short Stories

Before Eden

"I guess," said Jerry Garfield, cutting the engines, "that this is the end of the line." With a gentle sigh, the underjets faded out; deprived of its air cushion, the scout car Rambling Wreck settled down upon the twisted rocks of the Hesperian Plateau.

There was no way forward; neither on its jets nor its tractors could S.5 – to give the Wreck its official name – scale the escarpment that lay ahead. The South Pole of Venus was only thirty miles away, but it might have been on another planet. They would have to turn back, and retrace their four-hundred-mile journey through this nightmare landscape.

The weather was fantastically clear, with visibility of almost a thousand yards. There was no need of radar to show the cliffs ahead; for once, the naked eye was good enough. The green auroral light, filtering down through clouds that had rolled unbroken for a million years, gave the scene an underwater appearance, and the way in which all distant objects blurred into the haze added to the impression. Sometimes it was easy to believe that they were driving across a shallow sea bed, and more than once Jerry had imagined that he had seen fish floating overhead.

"Shall I call the ship, and say we're turning back?" he asked.

"Not yet," said Dr. Hutchins. "I want to think."

Jerry shot an appealing glance at the third member of the crew, but found no moral support there. Coleman was just as bad; although the two men argued furiously half the time, they were both scientists and therefore, in the opinion of a hard-headed engineer-navigator, not wholly responsible citizens. If Cole and Hutch had bright ideas about going forward, there was nothing he could do except register a protest.

Hutchins was pacing back and forth in the tiny cabin, studying charts and instruments. Presently he swung the car's searchlight toward the cliffs, and began to examine them carefully with binoculars. Surely, thought Jerry, he doesn't expect me to drive up there! S.5 was a hover-track, not a mountain goat …

Abruptly, Hutchins found something. He released his breath in a sudden explosive gasp, then turned to Coleman.

"Look!" he said, his voice full of excitement. "Just to the left of that black mark! Tell me what you see."

He handed over the glasses, and it was Coleman's turn to stare.

"Well I'm damned," he said at length. "You were right. There are rivers on Venus. That's a dried-up waterfall."

"So you owe me one dinner at the Bel Gourmet when we get back to Cambridge. With champagne."

"So you owe me one dinner at the Bel Gourmet when we get back to Cambridge. With champagne."

"Just a minute," interjected Jerry. "What's all this about rivers and waterfalls? Everyone knows they can't exist on Venus. It never gets cold enough on this steam bath of a planet for the clouds to condense."

"Have you looked at the thermometer lately?" asked Hutchins with deceptive mildness.

"I've been slightly too busy driving."

"Then I've news for you. It's down to two hundred and thirty, and still falling. Don't forget – we're almost at the Pole, it's wintertime, and we're sixty thousand feet above the lowlands. All this adds up to a distinct nip in the air. If the temperature drops a few more degrees, we'll have rain. The water will be boiling, of course – but it will be water. And though George won't admit it yet, this puts Venus in a completely different light."

"Why?" asked Jerry, though he had already guessed.

—

"Where there's water, there may be life. We've been in too much of a hurry to assume that Venus is sterile, merely because the average temperature's over five hundred degrees. It's a lot colder here, and that's why I've been so anxious to get to the Pole. There are lakes up here in the highlands, and I want to look at them."

"But boiling water!" protested Coleman. "Nothing could live in that!"

"There are algae that manage it on Earth. And if we've learned one thing since we started exploring the planets, it's this: wherever life has the slightest chance of surviving, you'll find it. This is the only chance it's ever had on Venus."

"I wish we could test your theory. But you can see for yourself – we can't go up that cliff."

"Perhaps not in the car. But it won't be too difficult to climb those rocks, even wearing thermosuits. All we need do is walk a few miles toward the Pole; according to the radar maps, it's fairly level once you're over the rim. We could manage in – oh, twelve hours at the most. Each of us has been out for longer than that, in much worse conditions."

That was perfectly true. Protective clothing that had been designed to keep men alive in the Venusian lowlands would have an easy job here, where it was only a hundred degrees hotter than Death Valley in midsummer.

"Well," said Coleman, "you know the regulations. You can't go by yourself, and someone has to stay here to keep contact with the ship. How do we settle it this time – chess or cards?"

"Chess takes too long," said Hutchins, "especially when you two play it." He reached into the chart table and produced a well-worn pack. "Cut them, Jerry."

"Ten of spades. Hope you can beat it, George."

"So do I. Damn – only five of clubs. Well, give my regards to the

Venusians."

"So do I. Damn – only five of clubs. Well, give my regards to the Venusians."

They had climbed more than two thousand feet before the ground levelled out into a gentle slope, scarred here and there by channels that had clearly been cut by running water. After a little searching, they came across a gulley wide and deep enough to merit the name of river bed, and started to walk along it.

"I've just thought of something," said Jerry after they had travelled a few hundred yards. "Suppose there's a storm up ahead of us? I don't feel like facing a tidal wave of boiling water."

"If there's a storm," replied Hutchins a little impatiently, "we'll hear it. There'll be plenty of time to reach high ground."

He was undoubtedly right, but Jerry felt no happier as they continued to climb the gently shelving watercourse. His uneasiness had been growing ever since they had passed over the brow of the cliff and had lost radio contact with the scout car. In this day and age, to be out of touch with one's fellow men was a unique and unsettling experience. It had never happened to Jerry before in all his life; even aboard the Morning Star , when they were a hundred million miles from Earth, he could always send a message to his family and get a reply back within minutes. But now, a few yards of rock had cut him off from the rest of mankind; if anything happened to them here, no one would ever know, unless some later expedition found their bodies. George would wait for the agreed number of hours; then he would head back to the ship – alone. I guess I'm not really the pioneering type, Jerry told himself. I like running complicated machines, and that's how I got involved in space flight. But I never stopped to think where it would lead, and now it's too late to change my mind …

They had travelled perhaps three miles toward the Pole, following the meanders of the river bed, when Hutchins stopped to make observations and collect specimens. "Still getting colder!" he said. "The temperature's down to one hundred and ninety-nine. That's far and away the lowest ever recorded on Venus. I wish we could call

George and let him know."

Jerry tried all the wave bands; he even attempted to raise the ship – the unpredictable ups and downs of the planet's ionosphere sometimes made such long-distance reception possible – but there was not a whisper of a carrier wave above the roar and crackle of the Venusian thunderstorms.

"This is even better," said Hutchins, and now there was real excitement in his voice. "The oxygen concentration's way up – fifteen parts in a million. It was only five back at the car, and down in the lowlands you can scarcely detect it."

"But fifteen in a million! " protested Jerry. "Nothing could breathe that!"

"You've got hold of the wrong end of the stick," Hutchins explained. "Nothing does breathe it.

Something makes it. Where do you think Earth's oxygen comes from? It's all produced by life – by growing plants. Before there were plants on Earth, our atmosphere was just like this one – a mass of carbon dioxide and ammonia and methane. Then vegetation evolved, and slowly converted the atmosphere into something that animals could breathe."

Something makes it. Where do you think Earth's oxygen comes from? It's all produced by life – by growing plants. Before there were plants on Earth, our atmosphere was just like this one – a mass of carbon dioxide and ammonia and methane. Then vegetation evolved, and slowly converted the atmosphere into something that animals could breathe."

"It looks like it. Something not far from here is producing oxygen – and plant life is the simplest explanation."

"And where there are plants," mused Jerry, "I suppose you'll have animals, sooner or later."

"Yes," said Hutchins, packing his gear and starting up the gulley, "though it takes a few hundred million years. We may be too soon –

but I hope not."

"That's all very well," Jerry answered. "But suppose we meet something that doesn't like us? We've no weapons."

Hutchins gave a snort of disgust.

"And we don't need them. Have you stopped to think what we look like? Any animal would run a mile at the sight of us."

There was some truth in that. The reflecting metal foil of their thermosuits covered them from head to foot like flexible, glittering armour. No insects had more elaborate antennas than those mounted on their helmets and back packs, and the wide lenses through which they stared out at the world looked like blank yet monstrous eyes. Yes, there were few animals on Earth that would stop to argue with such apparitions; but any Venusians might have different ideas.

Jerry was still mulling this over when they came upon the lake. Even at that first glimpse, it made him think not of the life they were seeking, but of death. Like a black mirror, it lay amid fold of the hills; its far edge was hidden in the eternal mist, and ghostly columns of vapour swirled and danced upon its surface. All it needed, Jerry told himself, was Charon's ferry waiting to take them to the other side – or the Swan of Tuonela swimming majestically back and forth as it guarded the entrance to the Underworld …

Yet for all this, it was a miracle – the first free water that men had ever found on Venus. Hutchins was already on his knees, almost in an attitude of prayer. But he was only collecting drops of the precious liquid to examine through his pocket microscope.

"Anything there?" asked Jerry anxiously.

Hutchins shook his head.

"If there is, it's too small to see with this instrument. I'll tell you more when we're back at the ship." He sealed a test tube and placed it in his collecting bag, as tenderly as any prospector who had just found a nugget laced with gold. It might be – it probably was – nothing more than plain water. But it might also be a universe of unknown, living creatures on the first stage of their billion-year journey to intelligence.

Hutchins had walked no more than a dozen yards along the edge of the lake when he stopped again, so suddenly that Garfield nearly collided with him.

"What's the matter?" Jerry asked. "Seen something?"

"What's the matter?" Jerry asked. "Seen something?"

"What about it? It looks ordinary enough to me."

" I think it's grown bigger."

All his life, Jerry was to remember this moment. Somehow he never doubted Hutchins' statement; by this time he could believe anything, even that rocks could grow. The sense of isolation and mystery, the presence of that dark and brooding lake, the never-ceasing rumble of distant storms and the green flickering of the aurora – all these had done something to his mind, had prepared it to face the incredible. Yet he felt no fear; that would come later.

He looked at the rock. It was about five hundred feet away, as far as he could estimate. In this dim, emerald light it was hard to judge distances or dimensions. The rock – or whatever it was – seemed to be a horizontal slab of almost black material, lying near the crest of a low ridge. There was a second, much smaller, patch of similar material near it; Jerry tried to measure and memorise the gap between them, so that he would have some yardstick to detect any change.

Even when he saw that the gap was slowly shrinking, he still felt no alarm – only a puzzled excitement. Not until it had vanished completely, and he realised how his eyes had tricked him, did that awful feeling of helpless terror strike into his heart.
Here were no growing or moving rocks. What they were watching was a dark tide, a crawling carpet, sweeping slowly but inexorably toward them over the top of the ridge.

The moment of sheer, unreasoning panic lasted, mercifully, no more than a few seconds. Garfield's first terror began to fade as soon as he recognised its cause. For that advancing tide had reminded him, all too vividly, of a story he had read many years ago about the army ants of the Amazon, and the way in which they destroyed everything in their path …

But whatever this tide might be, it was moving too slowly to be a real danger, unless it cut off their line of retreat. Hutchins was staring at it intently through their only pair of binoculars; he was the biologist, and he was holding his ground. No point in making a fool of myself, thought Jerry, by running like a scalded cat, if it isn't necessary.

"For heaven's sake," he said at last, when the moving carpet was only a hundred yards away and Hutchins had not uttered a word or stirred a muscle. "What is it?"

Hutchins slowly unfroze, like a statue coming to life.

"Sorry," he said. "I'd forgotten all about you. It's a plant, of course. At least, I suppose we'd better call it that."

"But it's moving! "

"Why should that surprise you? So do terrestrial plants. Ever seen speeded-up movies of ivy in action?"

"That still stays in one place – it doesn't crawl all over the landscape."

"Then what about the plankton plants of the sea? They can swim when they have to."

"Then what about the plankton plants of the sea? They can swim when they have to."
He still thought of the thing as a carpet – a deep-pile one, ravelled into tassels at the edges. It varied in thickness as it moved; in some parts it was a mere film; in others, it heaped up to a depth of a foot or

more. As it came closer and he could see its texture, Jerry was reminded of black velvet. He wondered what it felt like to the touch, then remembered that it would burn his fingers even if it did nothing else to them. He found himself thinking, in the light-headed nervous reaction that often follows a sudden shock: "If there are any Venusians, we'll never be able to shake hands with them. They'd burn us, and we'd give them frostbite."

So far, the thing had shown no signs that it was aware of their presence. It had merely flowed forward like the mindless tide that it almost certainly was. Apart from the fact that it climbed over small obstacles, it might have been an advancing flood of water.

And then, when it was only ten feet away, the velvet tide checked itself. On the right and the left, it still flowed forward; but dead ahead it slowed to a halt.

"We're being encircled," said Jerry anxiously. "Better fall back, until we're sure it's harmless."

To his relief, Hutchins stepped back at once. After a brief hesitation, the creature resumed its flow advance and the dent in its front line straightened out.

Then Hutchins stepped forward again – and the thing slowly withdrew. Half a dozen times the biologist advanced, only to retreat again, and each time the living tide ebbed and flowed in synchronism with his movements. I never imagined, Jerry told himself, that I'd live to see a man waltzing with a plant …

"Thermophobia," said Hutchins. "Purely automatic reaction. It doesn't like our heat."

"Ourheat!" protested Jerry. "Why, we're living icicles by comparison."

"Of course – but our suits aren't, and that's all it knows about."
Stupid of me, thought Jerry. When you were snug and cool inside your thermosuit, it was easy to forget that the refrigeration unit on your back was pumping a blast of heat out into the surrounding air.

No wonder the Venusian plant had shied away …

"Let's see how it reacts to light," said Hutchins. He switched on his chest lamp, and the green auroral glow was instantly banished by the flood of pure white radiance. Until Man had come to this planet, no white light had ever shone upon the surface of Venus, even by day. As in the seas of Earth, there was only a green twilight, deepening slowly to utter darkness.

The transformation was so stunning that neither man could check a cry of astonishment. Gone in a flash was the deep, sombre black of the thick-piled velvet carpet at their feet. Instead, as far as their lights carried, lay a blazing pattern of glorious, vivid reds, laced with streaks of gold. No Persian prince could ever have commanded so opulent a tapestry from his weavers, yet this was the accidental product of biological forces. Indeed, until they had switched on their floods, these superb colours had not even existed, and they would vanish once more when the alien light of Earth ceased to conjure them into being.

"Tikov was right," murmured Hutchins. "I wish he could have known."

"Right about what?" asked Jerry, though it seemed almost a sacrilege to speak in the presence of such loveliness.

"Right about what?" asked Jerry, though it seemed almost a sacrilege to speak in the presence of such loveliness.

"You're sure it's quite safe?" asked Jerry, some of his caution reasserting itself.

"Absolutely – it can't touch our suits even if it wants to. Anyway, it's moving past us."

That was true. They could see now that the entire creature – if it was a single plant, and not a colony – covered a roughly circular area about a hundred yards across. It was sweeping over the ground, as the shadow of a cloud moves before the wind – and where it had rested, the rocks were pitted with innumerable tiny holes that might have been etched by acid.

"Yes," said Hutchins, when Jerry remarked about this. "That's how some lichens feed; they secrete acids that dissolve rock. But no questions, please – not till we get back to the ship. I've several lifetimes' work here, and a couple of hours to do it in."

This was botany on the run ... The sensitive edge of the huge plant-thing could move with surprising speed when it tried to evade them. It was as if they were dealing with an animated flapjack, an acre in extent. There was no reaction – apart from the automatic avoidance of their exhaust heat – when Hutchins snipped samples or took probes. The creature flowed steadily onward over hills and valleys, guided by some strange vegetable instinct. Perhaps it was following some vein of mineral; the geologists could decide that, when they analysed the rock samples that Hutchins had collected both before and after the passage of the living tapestry.

There was scarcely time to think or even to frame the countless questions that their discovery had raised. Presumably these creatures must be fairly common, for them to have found one so quickly. How did they reproduce? By shoots, spores, fission, or some other means? Where did they get their energy? What relatives, rivals, or parasites did they have? This could not be the only form of life on Venus – the very idea was absurd, for if you had one species, you must have thousands ...

Sheer hunger and fatigue forced them to a halt at last. The creature they were studying could eat its way around Venus – though Hutchins believed that it never went very far from the lake, as from time to time it approached the water and inserted a long, tubelike tendril into it – but the animals from Earth had to rest.

It was a great relief to inflate the pressurised tent, climb in through the air lock, and strip off their thermosuits. For the first time, as they relaxed inside their tiny plastic hemisphere, the true wonder and importance of the discovery forced itself upon their minds. This world around them was no longer the same; Venus was no longer dead – it had joined Earth and Mars.

For life called to life, across the gulfs of space. Everything that grew

---

or moved upon the face of any planet was a portent, a promise that Man was not alone in this universe of blazing suns and swirling nebulae. If as yet he had found no companions with whom he could speak, that was only to be expected, for the light-years and the ages still stretched before him, waiting to be explored. Meanwhile, he must guard and cherish the life he found, whether it be upon Earth or Mars or Venus.

So Graham Hutchins, the happiest biologist in the solar system, told himself as he helped Garfield collect their refuse and seal it into a plastic disposal bag. When they deflated the tent and started on the homeward journey, there was no sign of the creature they had been examining. That was just as well; they might have been tempted to linger for more experiments, and already it was getting uncomfortably close to their deadline.

So Graham Hutchins, the happiest biologist in the solar system, told himself as he helped Garfield collect their refuse and seal it into a plastic disposal bag. When they deflated the tent and started on the homeward journey, there was no sign of the creature they had been examining. That was just as well; they might have been tempted to linger for more experiments, and already it was getting uncomfortably close to their deadline.

For a while nothing moved in the greenly glimmering, fog-bound landscape; it was deserted by man and crimson carpet alike. Then, flowing over the wind-carved hills, the creature reappeared. Or perhaps it was another of the same strange species; no one would ever know.

It flowed past the little cairn of stones where Hutchins and Garfield had buried their wastes. And then it stopped.

It was not puzzled, for it had no mind. But the chemical urges that drove it relentlessly over the polar plateau were crying: Here, here! Somewhere close at hand was the most precious of all the foods it needed – phosphorous, the element without which the spark of life could never ignite. It began to nuzzle the rocks, to ooze into the cracks and crannies, to scratch and scrabble with probing tendrils. Nothing that it did was beyond the capacity of any plant or tree on

Earth – but it moved a thousand times more quickly, requiring only minutes to reach its goal and pierce through the plastic film.

And then it feasted, on food more concentrated than any it had ever known. It absorbed the carbohydrates and the proteins and the phosphates, the nicotine from the cigarette ends, the cellulose from the paper cups and spoons. All these it broke down and assimilated into its strange body, without difficulty and without harm.

Likewise it absorbed a whole microcosm of living creatures – the bacteria and viruses which, upon an older planet, had evolved into a thousand deadly strains. Though only a very few could survive in this heat and this atmosphere, they were sufficient. As the carpet crawled back to the lake, it carried contagion to all its world.

Even as theMorning Star set its course for her distant home, Venus was dying. The films and photographs and specimens that Hutchins was carrying in triumph were more precious even than he knew. They were the only record that would ever exist of life's third attempt to gain a foothold in the solar system.

Beneath the clouds of Venus, the story of Creation was ended.

Exile of the Eons

Already the mountains were trembling with the thunder that only man can make. But here the war seemed very far away, for the full moon hung over The Himalayas and the blinding furies of the battle were still hidden below the edge of the world. Not for long would they remain. The Master knew that the last remnants of his fleet were being hurled from the sky as the circle of death closed swiftly on his stronghold.

In a few hours at the most, the Master and his dreams of empire would have vanished into the past. Nations would still curse his name, but they would no longer fear it. Later, even the hatred would be gone and he would mean no more to the world than Hitler or Napoleon or Genghis Khan. Like them he would be a blurred figure far down the infinite corridor of time, dwindling toward oblivion.

Far to the south, a mountain was suddenly edged with violet flame. Ages later, the balcony on which the Master stood shuddered beneath the impact of the ground wave racing through the rocks below. Later still, the air brought the echo to a mammoth concussion. Surely they could not be so close already! The Master hoped it was no more than a stray torpedo that had swept through the contracting battle line. If it were not, time was even shorter than he feared. Thee Chief ot Staff walked out from the shadows and joined him by the rail. The Marshal's hard face -- the second most hated in all the world -- was lined and beaded with sweat. He had not slept for many days and his once gaudy uniform hung limply upon him. Yet his eyes, though unutterably weary, were still resolute even in defeat. He stood in silence, awaiting his last orders. Nothing else was left for him to do.

Thirty miles away, the eternal snow-plume of Everest flamed a lurid red, reflecting the glare of some colossal fire below the horizon. Still the Master neither moved nor gave any sign. Not until a salvo of torpedoes passed high overhead with a demon wail did he turn and, with one backward glance at the world he would see no more, descend into the depths.

The lift dropped a thousand feet and the sound of battle died away. As he stepped out of the shaft, the Master paused for a moment to press a hidden switch. The Marshal smiled when he heard the crash of falling rock far above, and knew that pursuit and escape were equally impossible.

As of old, the handful of generals sprang to their feet when the Master entered the room. He walked to his place in silence, steeling himself for the last and hardest speech he would ever have to make. Burning into his soul he could feel the eyes of the men he had led to ruin. Behind and beyond them he could see the squadrons, the divisions, the armies whose blood was on his hands. And more terrible still were the silent specters of the nations that now could never be born.

At last he began to speak. The hypnosis of his voice was as powerful as ever, and after a few words he became once more the perfect, implacable machine whose destiny was destruction.

"This, gentlemen, is the last of all our meetings. There are no more plans to make, no more maps to study. Somewhere above our heads the fleet we built with such pride and care is fighting to the end. In a few minutes, not one of all those thousands of machines will be left in the sky. "I know that for all of us here surrender is unthinkable, even if it were possible, so in this room you will shortly have to die. You have served our cause and deserved better, but it was not to be. Yet I do not wish you to think that we have wholly failed. In the past, as you saw many times, my plans were always ready for everything that might arise, no matter how improbable. You should not, therefore, be surprised to learn that I was prepared even for defeat."

Still the same superb orator, he paused for effect, noting with satisfaction the ripple of interest, the sudden alertness on the tired faces of his listeners.

"My secret is safe enough with you," he continued, "for the enemy will never find this place. The entrance is already blocked by many hundreds of feet of rock."

Still there was no movement. Only the Director of Propaganda turned suddenly white, and swiftly recovered -- but not swiftly enough to escape the Master's eye. The Master smiled inwardly at this belated confirmation of an old doubt. It mattered little now; true and false, they would all die together.

All but one.

"Two years ago," he went on, "when we lost the battle of Antarctica, I knew that we could no longer be certain of victory. So I made my preparations for this day. The enemy has already sworn to kill me. I could not remain in hiding anywhere on the Earth, still less hope to rebuild our fortunes.

"But there is another way, though a desperate one.

"Five years ago, one of our scientists perfected the technique of suspended animation. He found that by relatively simple means all life processes could be arrested for an indefinite time. I am going to use this discovery to escape from the present into a future which will have forgotten me. There I can begin the struggle again, with the help of certain devices that might yet have won this war had we been granted more time.

"Good-by, gentlemen. And once again, my thanks for your help and my regrets at your ill fortune."

He saluted, turned on his heel, and was gone. The Metal door thudded decisively behind him. There was a frozen silence; then the Director of Propaganda rushed to the exit, only to recoil with a startled cry. The steel door was already too hot to touch. It had been welded immovably into the wall.

The Minister for War was the first to draw his automatic.

The Master was in no great hurry now. On leaving the council room he had thrown the secret switch of the welding circuit. The same action had opened a panel in the wall of the corridor, revealing a small circular passage sloping steadily upward. He began to walk slowly along it.

Every few hundred feet the tunnel angled sharply, though still continuing the upward climb. At each turning the Master stopped to throw a switch, and there was the thunder of falling rock as a section of corridor collapsed.

Five times the passageway changed its course before it ended in a spherical, metal-walled room. Multiple doors closed softly on rubber seatings, and the last section of tunnel crashed behind. The Master would not be disturbed by his enemies, nor by his friends.

He looked swiftly around the room to satisfy himself that all was ready. Then he walked to a simple control board and threw, one after another, a set of tiny switches. They had to carry little current -- but they had been built to last. So had everything in that strange room. Even the walls were made of metals far less ephemeral than steel.

Pumps started to whine, drawing the air from the chamber and replacing it with sterile nitrogen. Moving more swiftly now, the Master went to the padded couch and lay down. He thought he could feel himself bathed by the bacteria-destroying rays from the lamps above his head, but that of course was fancy. From a recess beneath the couch he drew a hypodermic and injected a milky fluid into his arm. Then he relaxed and waited.

It was already very cold. Soon the refrigerators would bring the temperature down far below freezing, and would hold it there for many hours. Then it would rise to normal, but by that time the process would be completed, all bacteria would be dead and the Master could sleep, unchanged, forever.

He had planned to wait a hundred years. More than that he dared not delay, for when he awoke he would have to master all the changes in science and society that the passing years had wrought. Even a century might have altered the face of a civilization beyond his understanding, but that was a risk he would have to take. Less than a century would not be safe, for the world would still be full of bitter memories.

Sealed in a vacuum beneath the couch were the electronic counters operated by thermocouples hundreds of feet above, on the eastern face of the mountain where no snow could ever cling. Every day the rising sun would operate them and the counters would add one unit to their store. So the coming of dawn would be noted in the darkness where the Master slept.

When any one of the counters reached the total of thirty-six thousand, a switch would close and oxygen would flow back into the chamber. The temperature would rise, and the automatic hypodermic strapped to the Master's arm would inject the calculated amount of fluid. He would awaken. Then he would press the button which would blast away the mountainside and give him free passage to the outer world.

Everything had been considered. There could be no failure. All the machinery had been triplicated and was as perfect as science could contrive.

The Master's last thought as consciousness ebbed was not of his past life, nor of the mother whose hopes he had betrayed. Unbidden and unwelcome, there came into his mind the words of an ancient poet:

To sleep, perchance to dream . . . No, he would not, he dared not dream. He would only sleep . . . sleep . . . sleep. . .

Twenty miles away, the battle was coming to its end. Not a dozen of the Master's ships were left, fighting hopelessly against overwhelming fire. The action would have ended long ago had the attackers not been ordered to risk no ships in unnecessary adventures. The decision was to be left to the long-range artillery. So the great destroyers, the airborne battleships of this age, lay with their fighter screens in the shelter of the mountains, pouring salvo after salvo into the doomed formations.

Aboard the flagship, a young Hindu gunnery officer set vernier dials with infinite care and gently pressed a pedal with his foot. There was the faintest of shocks as the dirigible torpedoes left their cradles and hurled themselves at the enemy. The young Indian sat waiting tensely as the chronometer ticked off the seconds. This, he thought, was probably the last salvo he would ever fire. Somehow he felt none of the elation he had expected; indeed, he was surprised to discover a kind of impersonal sympathy for his doomed opponents, whose lives were now ebbing with every passing second.

Far away a sphere of violet fire blossomed above the mountains, among the darting specks that were enemy ships. The gunner leaned forward tensely and counted. One-two-three-four-five times came that peculiar explosion. Then the sky cleared. The struggling specks were gone.

In his log, the gunner noted briefly: "0124 hrs. Salvo No. 12 fired. Five torps exploded among enemy ships, which were destroyed. One torp failed to detonate."

He signed the entry with a flourish and laid down his pen. For a while he sat staring at the log's familiar brown cover, with the cigarette burns at the edges and the inevitable stained rings where cups and.glasses had been carelessly set down. Idly he thumbed through the leaves, noting once again the handwriting of his many predecessors. And as he had done so often before, he turned to a familiar page where a man who had once been his friend had begun to sign his name but had never lived to complete it.

With a sigh, he closed the book and locked it away. The war was over.

Far away among the mountains, the torpedo that had failed to explode was still gaining speed under the drive of its rockets. Now it was a scarcely visible line of light, racing between the walls of a lonely valley. Already the snows that had been disturbed by the scream of its passage were beginning to rumble down the mountain slopes.

There was no escape from the valley: it was blocked by a sheer wall a thousand feet high. Here the torpedo that had missed its mark found a greater one. The Master's tomb was too deep in the mountain even to be shaken by the explosion but the hundreds of tons of falling rock swept away three tiny instruments and their connections, and a future that might have been went with them into oblivion.

The first rays of the rising sun would still fall on the shattered face of the mountain, but the counters that were waiting for the thirty-six thousandth dawn would still be waiting when dawns and sunsets were no more.

In the silence of the tomb that was not quite a tomb, the Master knew nothing of this. And he slumbered on, until the century was far behind -- very far indeed.

After what by some standards would have been a little while, the earth's crust decided it had borne the weight of The Himalayas for long enough. Slowly the mountains dropped, tilting the southern plains of India toward the sky. And presently the plateau of Ceylon was the highest point on the surface of the globe, and the ocean about Everest was five and a half miles deep. Yet the Master's slumber was still dreamless and undisturbed.

Slowly, patiently, the silt drifted down through the towering ocean heights onto the wreck of The Himalayas. The blanket that would one day be chalk began to thicken at the rate of an inch or two every century. If one had returned some time later, one might have found that the sea bed was no longer five miles down, or even four, or three. Then the land tilted again, and a mighty range of limestone mountains towered where once had been the oceans of Tibet. But the Master knew nothing of this, nor was his sleep troubled when it happened again and again and yet again.

Now the rain and the rivers were washing away the chalk and carrying it out to the strange new oceans, and the surface was moving down toward the hidden tomb. Slowly the miles of rock were winnowed away until at last the sphere which housed the Master's body returned to the light of day -- though to a day much longer, and much dimmer, than it had been when the Master closed his eyes.

Little did the Master dream of the races that had flowered and died since that early morning of the world when he went to his long sleep. Very far away was that morning now, and the shadows were lengthening to the east; the sun was dying and the world was very old. But still the children of Adam ruled its seas and skies, and filled with their tears and laughter the plains and the valleys and the woods that were older than the shifting hills.

The Master's dreamless sleep was more than half ended when Trevindor the Philosopher was born, between the fall of the Ninety-seventh Dynasty and the rise of the Fifth Galactic Empire. He was born on a world very far from Earth. Few were the men who now set foot on the ancient home of their race, so distant from the throbbing heart of the Universe.

They brought Trevindor to Earth when his brief clash with the Empire had come to its inevitable end. Here he was tried by the men whose ideals he had challenged, and here it was that they pondered long over the manner of his necessary fate.

The case was unique. The gentle, philosophic culture that now ruled the Galaxy had never before met with opposition, even on the level of pure intellect, and the polite but implacable conflict of wills had left it severe- ly shaken. It was typical of the council's members when a decision had proved impossible, they had appealed to Trevindor himself for help.

In the whitely gleaming Hall of Justice, that had not been entered for nigh on a million years, Trevindor stood proudly facing the men who had proved stronger than he. In silence he listened to their request; then he paused in reflection. His judges waited patiently until at last he spoke.

"You suggest that I should promise not to defy you again," he began, "but I shall make no promise that I may be unable to keep. Our views are too divergent and sooner or later we should clash again.

"There was a time when your choice would have been easy. You could have exiled me, or put me to death. But today -- where among all the worlds of the Universe is there one planet where you could hide me if I did not choose to stay? Remember, I have many disciples scattered the length and breadth of the Galaxy.

"There remains the other alternative. I shall bear you no malice if you revive the ancient custom of execution to meet my case."

There was a murmur of annoyance from the Council, and the President replied sharply, his color heightening.

"That remark is in questionable taste. We asked for serious suggestions, not reminders -- even if intended humorously -- of the barbaric customs of our remote ancestors."

Trevindor accepted the rebuke with a bow. "I was merely mentioning all the possibilities. There are two others that have occurred to me. It would be a simple matter to change my mind pattern to your way of thinking so that no future disagreement can arise."

"We have already considered that. We were forced to reject it, attractive though it is, for the destruction of your personality would be equivalent to murder. There are only fifteen more powerful intellects than yours in the Universe, and we have no right to tamper with it. And your final suggestion?"

"Though you cannot exile me in space, there is still one alternative. The river of Time stretches ahead of us as far as pur thoughts can go. Send me down that stream to an age when you are certain this civilization will have passed. That I know you can do with the aid of the Roston time-field."

There was a long pause. In silence the members of the Council were passing their decisions to the complex analysis machine which would weigh them one against the other and arrive at the verdict. At length the President spoke.

"It is agreed. We will send you to an age when the sun is still warm enough for life to exist on the Earth, but so remote that any trace of our civilization is unlikely to survive. We will also provide you with everything necessary for your safety and reasonable comfort. You may leave us now. We will call for you again as soon as all arrangements have been made."

Trevindor bowed, and left the marble hall. No guards followed him. There was nowhere he could flee, even if he wished, in this Universe which the great Galactic liners could span in a single day.

For the first and the last time, Trevindor stood on the shore of what had once been the Pacific, listening to the wind sighing through the leaves of what had once been palms. The few stars of the nearly empty region of space through which the sun was now passing shone with a steady light through the dry air of the aging world. Trevindor wondered bleakly if they would still be shining when he looked again upon the sky, in a future so distant that the sun itself would be sinking to its death.

There was a tinkle from the tiny communicator band upon his wrist. So, the time had come. He turned his back upon the ocean and walked resolutely to meet his fate. Before he had gone a dozen steps, the time-field had seized him and his thoughts froze in an instant that would remain unchanged while the oceans shrank and vanished, the Galactic Empire passed away, and the great star clusters crumbled into nothingness.

But, to Trevindor, no time elapsed at all. He only knew that at one step there had been moist sand beneath his feet, and at the next hard, baked rock. The palms had vanished, the murmur of the sea was stilled. It needed only a glance to show that even the memory of the sea had long since faded from this parched and dying world. To the far horizon, a great desert of red sandstone stretched unbroken and unrelieved by any growing thing. Overhead, the orange disk of a strangely altered sun glowered from a sky so black that many stars were clearly visible.

Yet, it seemed, there was still life on this ancient world. To the north -- if that were still the north -- the somber light glinted upon some metallic structure. It was a few hundred yards away, and as Trevindor started to walk toward it he was conscious of a curious lightness, as if gravity itself had weakened.

He had not gone far before he saw that he was approaching a low metal building which seemed to have been set down on the plain rather than constructed there, for it tilted slightly with the slope of the land. Trevindor wondered at his incredible good fortune at finding civilization so easily. Another dozen steps, and he realized that not chance but design had so conveniently placed this building here, and that it was as much a stranger to this world as he himself.

There was no hope at all that anyone would come to meet him as he walked toward it.

The metal plaque above the door added little to whal he had already surmised. Still new and untarnished as if it had just been engraved -- as indeed, in a sense, it had -- the lettering brought a message at once of hope and of bitterness.

To Trevindor, the greetings of the Council.

This building, which we have sent after you through the time-field, will supply all your needs for an indefinite period.

We do not know if civilization will still exist in the age in which you find yourself. Man may now be extinct, since the chromosome K Star K will have become dominant and the race may have mutated into something no longer human. That is for you to discover.

You are now in the twilight of the Earth and it is our hope that you are not alone. But if it is your destiny to be the last living creature on this once lovely world, remember that the choice was yours. Farewell.

Twice Trevindor read the message, recognizing with an ache the closing words which could only have been written by his friend, the poet Cintillarne. An overwhelming sense of loneliness and isolation came flooding into his soul. He sat down upon a shelf of rock and buried his face in his hands.

A long time later, he arose to enter the building. He felt more than grateful to the long-dead Council which had treated him so chivalrously. The technical achievement of sending an entire building through time was one he had believed beyond the resources of his age. A sudden thought struck him and he glanced again at the engraved lettering, noticing for the first time the date it bore. It was five thousand years later than the time when he had faced his peers in the Hall of Justice.

Fifty centuries had passed before his judges could redeem their promise to a man as good as dead. Whatever the faults of the

Council, its integrity was of an order beyond the comprehension of an earlier age.

Many days passed before Trevindor left the building again. Nothing had been overlooked: even his beloved thought records were there. He could continue to study the nature of reality and to construct philosophies until the end of the Universe, barren though that occupation would be if his were the only mind left on Earth. There was little danger, he thought wryly, that his speculations concerning the purpose of human existence would once again bring him into conflict with society.

Not until he had investigated the building thoroughly did Trevindor turn his attention once more to the outer world. The supreme problem was that of contacting civilization, should such still exist. He had been provided with a powerful receiver, and for hours he wandered up and down the spectrum in the hope of discovering a station. The far-off crackle of static came from the instrument and once there was a burst of what might have been speech in a tongue that was certainly not human. But nothing else rewarded his search. The ether, which had been man's faithful servant for so many ages, was silent at last.

The little automatic flyer was Trevindor's sole remaining hope. He had what was left of eternity before him, and Earth was a small planet. In a few years at the most, he could have explored it all.

So the months passed while the exile began his methodical exploration of the world, returning ever and again to his home in the desert of red sandstone.

Everywhere he found the same picture of desolation and ruin. How long ago the seas had vanished he could not even guess, but in their dying they had left endless wastes of salt, encrusting both plains and mountains with a blanket of dirty gray.

Trevindor felt glad that he had not been born on Earth and so had never known it in the glory of its youth. Stranger though he was, the loneliness and desolation of the world chilled his heart; had he lived here before, its sadness would have been unbearable.

Thousands of square miles of desert passed beneath Trevindor's fleeting ship as he searched the world from pole to pole. Only once did he find any sign that Earth had ever known civilization. In a deep valley near the equator he discovered the ruins of a small city of strange white stone and stranger architecture. The buildings were perfectly preserved, though half buried by the drifting sand, and for a moment Trevindor felt a surge of somber joy at the knowledge that man had, after all, left some traces of his handiwork on the world that had been his first home.

The emotion was short-lived. The buildings were stranger than Trevindor had realized, for no man could ever have entered them. Their only openings were wide, horizontal slots close to the ground; there were no windows of any kind. Trevindor's mind reeled as he tried to imagine the creatures that must have occupied them. In spite of his growing loneliness, he felt glad that the dwellers in this inhuman city had passed away so long before his time. He did not linger here, for the bitter night was almost upon him and the valley filled him with an oppression that was not entirely rational.

And once, he actually discovered life. He was cruising over the bed of one of the lost oceans when a flash of color caught his eye. Upon a knoll which the drifting sand had not yet buried was a thin, wiry covering of grass. That was all, but the sight brought tears to his eyes.

He grounded the machine and stepped out, treading warily lest he destroy even one of the struggling blades. Tenderly he ran his hands over the threadbare carpet which was all the life that Earth now knew. Before he left, he sprinkled the spot with as much water as he could spare. It was a futile gesture, but one which made him feel happier.

The search was now nearly completed. Trevindor had long ago given up all hope, but his indomitable spirit still drove him on across the face of the world. He could not rest until he had proved what as yet he only feared. And thus it was that he came at last to the Master's tomb as it lay gleaming dully in the sunlight from which it had been banished so unthinkably long.

The Master's mind awoke before his body. As he lay powerless, unable even to lift his eyelids, memory came flooding back. The hundred years were safely behind him. His gamble, the most desperate that any man had ever made, had succeeded! An immense weariness came over him and for a while consciousness faded once more.

Presently the mists cleared again and he felt stronger, though still too weak to move. He lay in the darkness gathering his strength together. What sort of a world, he wondered, would he find when he stepped forth from the mountainside into the light of day? Would he be able to put his plans into -- ? What was that? A spasm of sheer terror shook the very foundations of his mind, Something was moving beside him, here in the tomb where nothing should be stirring but himself.

Then, calm and clear, a thought rang through his mind and quelled in an instant the fears that had threatened to overturn it.

"Do not be alarmed. I have come to help you. You are safe, and everything will be well."

The Master was too stunned to make any reply, bul his subconscious must have formulated some sort of answer, for the thought came again.

"That is good. I am Trevindor, like yourself an exile in this world. Do not move, but tell me how you came here and what is your race, for I have seen none like it."

And now fear and caution were creeping back into the Master's mind. What manner of creature was this that could read his thoughts, and what was it doing in his secret sphere? Again that clear, cold thought echoed through his brain like the tolling of a bell.

"Once more I tell you that you have nothing to fear. Why are you alarmed because I can see into your mind? Surely there is nothing strange in that."

"Nothing strange!" cried the Master. "Who are you -- what are you, for God's sake?"

"A man like yourself. But your race must be primitive indeed if the reading of thoughts is foreign to you."

A terrible suspicion began to dawn in the Master's brain. The answer came even before he consciously framed the question.

"You have slept infinitely longer than a hundred years. The world you knew has ceased to be for longer than you can imagine."

The Master heard no more. Once again the darkness swept over him and he sank down into unconsciousness.

In silence Trevindor stood by the couch on which the Master lay. He was filled with an elation which for the moment outweighed any disappointment he might feel. At least, he would no longer have to face the future alone. All the terror of the Earth's loneliness, that was weighing so heavily upon his soul, had vanished in a moment. No longer alone ... no longer alone!

The Master was beginning to stir once more, and into Trevindor's mind crept broken fragments of thought. Pictures of the world the Master had known began to form. At first Trevindor could make nothing of them; then, suddenly, the jumbled shards fell into place. A wave of horror swept over him at the appalling vista of nation battling against nation, of cities flaming to destruction. What kind of world was this? Could man have sunk so low from the peaceful age Trevindor had known? There had been legends of such things, from times incredibly remote, but man had left them with his childhood. Surely they could never have returned!

The broken thoughts were more vivid now, and even more horrible. It was truly a nightmare age from which this other exile had come -- no wonder that he had fled from itl

Suddenly the truth began to dawn in the mind of Trevindor as, sick at heart, he watched the ghastly patterns passing through the Master's brain. This was no exile seeking refuge from an age of horror. This was the very creator of that horror, who had embarked on the river of time with one purpose alone -- to spread contagion down to later years.

Passions that Trevindor had never imagined began to parade themselves before his eyes: ambition, the lust for power, cruelty, intolerance, hatred. He tried to close his mind, but found he had lost the power to do so. With a cry of anguish, Trevindor rushed out into the silent desert.

It was night, and very still, for the Earth was now too weary even for winds to blow. The darkness hid everything, but Trevindor knew that it could not hide the thoughts of that other mind with which he now must share the world. Once he had been alone, and he had imagined nothing more dreadful. But now he knew that there were things more fearful even than solitude.

The stillness of the night, and the glory of the stars that had once been his friends, brought calm to the soul of Trevindor. Slowly he turned and retraced his footsteps, walking heavily, for he was about to perform a deed that no man of his kind had ever done before.

The Master was erect when Trevindor re-entered the sphere. Perhaps some hint of the other's purpose dawned upon his mind, for he was very pale. Steadfastly, Trevindor forced himself to look once more into the Master's brain. His mind recoiled at the chaos of conflicting emotions, now shot through with sickening flashes of fear. Out of the maelstrom one coherent thought came timidly quavering.

"What are you going to do? Why do you look at me like that?"

Trevindor made no reply, holding his mind aloof from contamination while he marshaled his resolution and all his strength.

The tumult in the Master's mind was rising to crescendo. For a moment his mounting terror brought something akin to pity to the gentle spirit of Trevindor, and his will faltered. But then there came again the picture of those ruined and burning cities.

With all the power of his intellect, backed by thousands of centuries of mental evolution, he struck at the man before him. Into the Master's mind, obliterating all else, flooded the single thought of -- death.

For a moment the Master stood motionless, his eyes staring wildly. His breath froze as his lungs ceased their work; in his veins the pulsing blood, which had been stilled for so long, now congealed forever.

Without a sound, the Master toppled and lay still.

Very slowly Trevindor turned and walked out into the night. Like a shroud the silence and loneliness of the world descended upon him. The sand, thwarted so long, began to drift through the open portals of the Master's tomb.

The Nine Billion Names of God

The title story was written, for want of anything better to do, during a rainy weekend at the Roosevelt Hotel. Its basic arithmetic was later challenged by J. B. S. Haldane , but I managed to save the situation by alphanumeric evasions whose precise nature now escapes me.

"J. B. S." also remarked of this story, and "The Star" (q.v.): "You are one of the very few living persons who has written anything original about God. You have in fact written several mutually incompatible things. If you had stuck to one theological hypothesis you might have been a serious public danger." I am glad of my self-contradiction, preferring to remain a prophet with a small p.

Nevertheless, I appear to have created a durable myth: not long ago, a radio talk on the BBC referred to the opening situation of this story as actual fact. And now that IBM computers have entered the field of biblical scholarship, perhaps this theme iscoming a little closer to reality.

"This is a slightly unusual request," said Dr. Wagner, with what he hoped was commendable restraint. "As far as I know, it's the first time anyone's been asked to supply a Tibetan monastery with an Automatic Sequence Computer. I don't wish to be inquisitive, but I should hardly have thought that your -ah-establishment had much use for such a machine. Could you explain just what you intend to do with it?"

"Gladly," replied the lama, readjusting his silk robes and carefully putting away the slide rule he had been using for currency conversions. "Your Mark V Computer can carry out any routine mathematical operation involving up to ten digits. However, for our work we are interested in letters, not numbers. As we wish you to modify the output circuits, the machine will be printing words, not columns of figures."

"Gladly," replied the lama, readjusting his silk robes and carefully putting away the slide rule he had been using for currency conversions. "Your Mark V Computer can carry out any routine mathematical operation involving up to ten digits. However, for our work we are interested in letters, not numbers. As we wish you to modify the output circuits, the machine will be printing words, not columns of figures."

"This is a project on which we have been working for the last three centuries-since the lamasery was founded, in fact. It is somewhat alien to your way of thought, so I hope you will listen with an open mind while I explain it."

"Naturally."

"It is really quite simple. We have been compiling a list which shall contain all the possible names of God."

"I beg your pardon?"

"We have reason to believe," continued the lama imper-turbably , "that all such names can be written with not more than nine letters in an alphabet we have devised."

"And you have been doing this for three centuries?"

"Yes: we expected it would take us about fifteen thousand years to complete the task."

"Oh," Dr. Wagner looked a little dazed. "Now I see why you wanted to hire one of our machines. But exactly what is the purpose of this project?"

The lama hesitated for a fraction of a second, and Wagner wondered if he had offended him. If so, there was no trace of annoyance in the reply.

"Call it ritual, if you like, but it's a fundamental part of our belief. All the many names of the Supreme Being-God, Jehovah, Allah, and so on-they are only man-made labels. There is a philosophical problem of some difficulty here, which I do not propose to discuss, but somewhere among all the possible combinations of letters that can occurare what one may call the real names of God. By systematic permutation of letters, we have been trying to list them all."

"Call it ritual, if you like, but it's a fundamental part of our belief. All the many names of the Supreme Being-God, Jehovah, Allah, and so on-they are only man-made labels. There is a philosophical problem of some difficulty here, which I do not propose to discuss, but somewhere among all the possible combinations of letters that can occurare what one may call the real names of God. By systematic permutation of letters, we have been trying to list them all."

"Exactly-though we use a special alphabet of our own. Modifying the electromatic typewriters to deal with this is, of course, trivial. A rather more interesting problem is that of devising suitable circuits to eliminate ridiculous combinations. For example, no letter must occur more than three times in succession."

"Three? Surely you mean two."

"Three is correct: I am afraid it would take too long to explain why, even if you understood our language."

"I'm sure it would," said Wagner hastily. "Go on."

"Luckily, it will be a simple matter to adapt your Automatic Sequence Computer for this work, since once it has been programed properly it will permute each letter in turn and print the result. What would have taken us fifteen thousand years it will be able to do in a hundred days."

Dr. Wagner was scarcely conscious of the faint sounds from theManhattan streets far below. He was in a different world, a world of natural, not man-made, mountains. High up in their remote aeries these monks had been patiently at work, generation after generation, compiling their lists of meaningless words. Was there any limit to the follies of mankind? Still, he must give no hint of his inner thoughts. The customer was always right. . . .

"There's no doubt," replied the doctor, "that we can modify the Mark V to print lists of this nature. I'm much more worried about the problem of installation and maintenance. Getting out toTibet , in these days, is not going to be easy."

"We can arrange that. The components are small enough to travel by air-that is one reason why we chose your machine. If you can get them toIndia , we will provide transport from there."

"We can arrange that. The components are small enough to travel by air-that is one reason why we chose your machine. If you can get them toIndia , we will provide transport from there."

"Yes, for the three months that the project should occupy."

"I've no doubt that Personnel can manage that." Dr. Wagner scribbled a note on his desk pad. "There are just two other points-"

Before he could finish the sentence the lama had produced a small slip of paper.

"This is my certified credit balance at the Asiatic Bank."

"Thank you. It appears to be-ah-adequate. The second matter is so trivial that I hesitate to mention it-but it's surprising how often the obvious gets overlooked. Whatsource of electrical energy have you?"

"A diesel generator providing fifty kilowatts at a hundred and ten volts.It was installed about five years ago and is quite reliable. It's made life at the lamasery much more comfortable, but of course it was really installed to provide power for the motors driving the prayer wheels."

"Of course," echoed Dr. Wagner. "I should have thought of that."

The view from the parapet was vertiginous, but in time one gets used to anything. After three months, George Hanley was not impressed by the two-thousand-foot swoop into the abyss or the remote checkerboard of fields in the valley below. He was leaning against the wind-smoothed stones and staring morosely at the distant mountains whose names he had never bothered to discover.

This, thought George, was the craziest thing that had ever happened to him. "Project Shangri-La," some wit back at the labs had christened it. For weeks now the Mark V had been churning out acres of sheets covered with gibberish. Patiently, inexorably, the computer had been rearranging letters in all their possible combinations, exhausting each class before going on to the next. As the sheets had emerged from the electromatic typewriters, the monks had carefully cut them up and pasted them into enormous books. In another week, heaven be praised, they would have finished. Just what obscure calculations had convinced the monks that they needn't bother to go on to words of ten, twenty, or a hundred letters, George didn't know. One of his recurring nightmares was that there would be some change of plan, and that the high lama (whom they'd naturally called Sam Jaffe, though he didn't look a bit like him) would suddenly announce that the project would be extended to approximately A.D. 2060. They were quite capable of it.

This, thought George, was the craziest thing that had ever happened to him. "Project Shangri-La," some wit back at the labs had christened it. For weeks now the Mark V had been churning out acres of sheets covered with gibberish. Patiently, inexorably, the computer had been rearranging letters in all their possible combinations, exhausting each class before going on to the next. As the sheets had emerged from the electromatic typewriters, the monks had carefully cut them up and pasted them into enormous books. In another week, heaven be praised, they would have finished. Just what obscure calculations had convinced the monks that they needn't bother to go on to words of ten, twenty, or a hundred letters, George didn't know. One of his recurring nightmares was that there would be some change of plan, and that the high lama (whom they'd naturally called Sam Jaffe, though he didn't look a bit like him) would suddenly announce that the project would be extended to approximately A.D. 2060. They were quite capable of it.

"Listen, George," said Chuck urgently. "I've learned something that means trouble."

"What's wrong? Isn't the machine behaving?" That was the worst contingency George could imagine. It might delay his return, and nothing could be more horrible. The way he felt now, even the sight of a TV commercial would seem like manna from heaven. At least it would be some link with home.

"No-it's nothing like that." Chuck settled himself on the parapet, which was unusual because normally he was scared of the drop. "I've just found what all this is about."

"What d'ya mean? I thought we knew."

"Sure-we know what the monks are trying to do. But we didn't know why. It's the craziest thing-"

"Tell me something new," growled George.

" But old Sam's just come clean with me. You know the way he drops in every afternoon to watch the sheets roll out. Well, this time he seemed rather excited, or at least as near as he'll ever get to it. When I told him that we were on the last cycle he asked me, in that cute English accent of his, if I'd ever wondered what they were trying to do. I said, 'Sure'- and he told me." told him that we were on the last cycle he asked me, in that cute English accent of his, if I'd ever wondered what they were trying to do. I said, 'Sure'- and he told me."

"Well, they believe that when they have listed all His names-and they reckon that there are about nine billion of them-God's purpose will be achieved. The human race will have finished what it was created to do, and there won't be any point in carrying on. Indeed, the very idea is something like blasphemy."

"Then what do they expect us to do? Commit suicide?"

"There's no need for that. When the list's completed, God steps in and simply winds things up . . . bingo!"

"Oh, I get it. When we finish our job, it will be the end of the world."

Chuck gave a nervous little laugh.

"That's just what I said to Sam. And do you know what happened? He looked at me in a very queer way, like I'd been stupid in class, and said, 'It's nothing as trivial as that.'"

George thought this over for a moment.

"That's what I call taking the Wide View," he said presently. "But what d'yousuppose we should do about it? I don't see that it makes the slightest difference to us. After all, we already knew that they were crazy."

"Yes-but don't you see what may happen? When thelist's complete and the Last Trump doesn't blow-or whatever it is they expect-we may get the blame. It's our machine they've been using. I don't like the situation one little bit."

"I see," said George slowly. "You've got a point there. But this sort of thing's happened before, you know. When I was a kid down inLouisiana we had a crackpot preacher who once said the world was going to end next Sunday. Hundreds of people believed him-even sold their homes. Yet when nothing happened, they didn't turn nasty, as you'd expect. They just decided that he'd made a mistake in his calculations andwent right on believing . I guess some of them still do."

"I see," said George slowly. "You've got a point there. But this sort of thing's happened before, you know. When I was a kid down inLouisiana we had a crackpot preacher who once said the world was going to end next Sunday. Hundreds of people believed him-even sold their homes. Yet when nothing happened, they didn't turn nasty, as you'd expect. They just decided that he'd made a mistake in his calculations andwent right on believing . I guess some of them still do."

"I've been wishing that for weeks. But there's nothing we can do until thecontract's finished and the transport arrives to fly us out."

"Of course," said Chuck thoughtfully, "we could always try a bit of sabotage."

"Like hell we could! That would make things worse." "Not the way I meant. Look at it like this. The machine

will finish its run four days from now, on the present twenty-hours-a-day basis. The transport calls in a week. OK-then all we need to do is to find something that needs replacing during one of the overhaul periods-something that will hold up the works for a couple of days. We'll fix it, of course, but not too quickly. If we time matters properly, we can be down at the airfield when the last name pops out of the register. They won't be able to catch us then."

"I don't like it," said George. "It will be the first time I ever walked out on a job. Besides, it would make them suspicious. No, I'll sit tight and take what comes."

"I still don't like it," he said, seven days later, as the tough little mountain ponies carried them down the winding road. "And don't you think I'm running away because I'm afraid. I'm just sorry for those poor old guys up there, and I don't want to be around when they find what suckers they've been. Wonder how Sam will take it?"

"It's funny," replied Chuck, "but when I said good-by I got the idea he knew we were walking out on him-and that he didn't care because he knew the machine was running smoothly and that the job would soon be finished. After that well, of course, for him there just isn't any AfterThat "

He knew exactly what was happening up on the mountain at this very moment. The high lama and his assistants would be sitting in their silk robes, inspecting the sheets as the junior monks carried them away from the typewriters and pasted them into the great volumes. No one would be saying anything. The only sound would be the incessant patter, the never-ending rainstorm of the keys hitting the paper, for the Mark V itself was utterly silent as it flashed through its thousands of calculations a second. Three months of this, thought George, was enough to start anyone climbing up the wall.

"There she is!" called Chuck, pointing down into the valley. " Ain't she beautiful! "

She certainly was, thought George. The battered old DC3 lay at the end of the runway like a tiny silver cross. In two hours she would be bearing them away to freedom and sanity. It was a thought worth savoring like a fine liqueur. George let it roll round his mind as the pony trudged patiently down the slope.

The swift night of the high Himalayas was now almost upon them. Fortunately, the road was very good, as roads went in that region, and they were both carrying torches. There was not the slightest danger, only a certain discomfort from the bitter cold. The sky overhead was perfectly clear, and ablaze with the familiar, friendly stars. At least there would be no risk, thought George, of the pilot being unable to take off because of weather conditions. That had been his only remaining worry.

He began to sing, but gave it up after a while. This vast arena of mountains, gleaming like whitely hooded ghosts on every side, did not encourage such ebullience. Presently George glanced at his watch.

"Should be there in an hour," he called back over his shoulder to Chuck. Then he added, in an afterthought: "Wonder if thecomputer's finished its run. It was due about now."

Chuck didn't reply, so George swung round in his saddle. He could just see Chuck's face, a white oval turned toward the sky.

If I Forget Thee, Oh Earth

When Marvin was ten years old, his father took him through the long, echoing corridors that led up through Administration and Power, until at last they came to the uppermost levels of all and were among the swiftly growing vegetation of the Farmlands. Marvin liked it here: it was fun watching the great, slender plants creeping with almost visible eagerness toward the sunlight as it filtered down through the plastic domes to meet them. The smell of life was everywhere, awakening inexpressible longings in his heart: no longer was he breathing the dry, cool air of the residential levels, purged of all smells but the faint tang of ozone. He wished he could stay here for a little while, but Father would not let him. They went onward until they had reached the entrance to the Observatory, which he had never visited: but they did not stop, and Marvin knew with a sense of rising excitement that there could be only one goal left. For the first time in his life, he was going Outside.

There were a dozen of the surface vehicles, with their wide balloon tires and pressurized cabins, in the great servicing chamber. His father must have been expected, for they were led at once to the little scout car waiting by the huge circular door of the airlock. Tense with expectancy, Marvin settled himself down in the cramped cabin while his father started the motor and checked the controls. The inner door of the lock slid open and then closed behind them: he heard the roar of the great air pumps fade slowly away as the Pressure dropped to zero. Then the "Vacuum" sign flashed on, the Outer door parted, and before Marvin lay the land which he had never yet entered.

He had seen it in photographs, of course: he had watched it imaged on television screens a hundred times. But now it was lying all around him, burning beneath the fierce sun that crawled so slowly across the jet-black sky. He stared into the west, away from the blinding splendor of the sun-and there were the stars, as he had been told but had never quite believed. He gazed at them for a long time, marveling that anything could be so bright and yet so tiny. They were intense unscintillating points, and suddenly he remembered a rhyme he had once read in one of his father's books:

Twinkle, twinkle, little star, How I wonder what you are.

Well, he knew what the stars were. Whoever asked that question must have been very stupid. And what did they mean by "twinkle"? You could see at a glance that all the stars shone with the same steady, unwavering light. He abandoned the puzzle and turned his attention to the landscape around him.

They were racing across a level plain at almost a hundred miles an hour, the great balloon tires sending up little spurts of dust behind them. There was no sign of the Colony: in the few minutes while he had been gazing at the stars, its domes and radio towers had fallen below the horizon. Yet there were other indications of man's presence, for about a mile ahead Marvin could see the curiously shaped structures clustering round the head of a mine. Now and then a puff of vapor would emerge from a squat smokestack and would instantly disperse.

They were past the mine in a moment: Father was driving with a reckless and exhilarating skill as if-it was a strange thought to come into a child's mind-he were trying to escape from something. In a few minutes they had reached the edge of the plateau on which the Colony had been built. The ground fell sharply away beneath them in a dizzying slope whose lower stretches were lost in shadow. Ahead, as far as the eye could reach, was a jumbled wasteland of craters, mountain ranges, and ravines. The crests of the mountains, catching the low sun, burned like islands of fire in a sea of darkness: and above them the stars still shone as steadfastly as ever.

There could be no way forward-yet there was. Marvin clenched his fists as the car edged over the slope and started the long descent. Then he saw the barely visible track leading down the mountain-side, and relaxed a little. Other men, it seemed, had gone this way before.

Night fell with a shocking abruptness as they crossed the shadow line and the sun dropped below the crest of the plateau. The twin searchlights sprang into life, casting blue-white bands on the rocks ahead, so that there was scarcely need to check their speed. For hours they drove through valleys and past the foot of mountains whose peaks seemed to comb the stars, and sometimes they emerged for a moment into the sunlight as they climbed over higher ground.

And now on the right was a wrinkled, dusty plain, and on the left, its ramparts and terraces rising mile after mile into the sky, was a wall of mountains that marched into the distance until its peaks sank from sight below the rim of the world. There was no sign that men had ever explored this land, but once they passed the skeleton of a crashed rocket, and beside it a stone cairn surmounted by a metal cross.

It seemed to Marvin that the mountains stretched on forever: but at last, many hours later, the range ended in a towering, precipitous headland that rose steeply from a cluster of little hills. They drove down into a shallow valley that curved in a great arc toward the far side of the mountains: and as they did so, Marvin slowly realized that something very strange was happening in the land ahead.

The sun was now low behind the hills on the right: the valley before them should be in total darkness. Yet it was awash with a cold white radiance that came spilling over the crags beneath which they were driving. Then, suddenly, they were out in the open plain, and the source of the light lay before them in all its glory.

It was very quiet in the little cabin now that the motors had stopped. The only sound was the faint whisper of the oxygen feed and an occasional metallic crepitation as the outer walls of the vehicle radiated away their heat. For no warmth at all came from the great silver crescent that floated low above the far horizon and flooded all this land with pearly light. It was so brilliant that minutes passed before Marvin could accept its challenge and look steadfastly into its glare, but at last he could discern the outlines of continents, the hazy border of the atmosphere, and the white islands of cloud.

And even at this distance, he could see the glitter of sunlight on the polar ice.

It was beautiful, and it called to his heart across the abyss of space. There in that shining crescent were all the wonders that he had never known-the hues of sunset skies, the moaning of the sea on pebbled shores, the patter of falling rain, the unhurried benison of snow. These and a thousand others should have been his rightful heritage, but he knew them only from the books and ancient records, and the thought filled him with the anguish of exile.

Why could they not return? It seemed so peaceful beneath those lines of marching cloud. Then Marvin, his eyes no longer blinded by the glare, saw that the portion of the disk that should have been in darkness was gleaming faintly with an evil phosphorescence: and he remembered. He was looking upon the funeral pyre of a world -upon the radioactive aftermath of Armageddon. Across a quarter of a million miles of space, the glow of dying atoms was still visible, a perennial reminder of the ruinous past. It would be centuries yet before that deadly glow died from the rocks and life could return again to fill that silent, empty world.

And now Father began to speak, telling Marvin the story which until this moment had meant no more to him than the fairy tales he had once been told. There were many things he could not understand: it was impossible for him to picture the glowing, multicolored pattern of life on the planet he had never seen. Nor could he comprehend the forces that had destroyed it in the end, leaving the Colony, preserved by its isolation, as the sole survivor. Yet he could share the agony of those final days, when the Colony had learned at last that never again would the supply ships come flaming down through the stars with gifts from home. One by one the radio stations had ceased to call: on the shadowed globe the lights of the cities had dimmed and died, and they were alone at last, as no men had ever been alone before, carrying in their hands the future of the race.

Then had followed the years of despair, and the long-drawn battle for survival in this fierce and hostile world. That battle had been won, though barely: this little oasis of life was safe against the worst that Nature could do. But unless there was a goal, a future toward which it could work, the Colony would lose the will to live, and neither machines nor skill nor science could save it then.

So, at last, Marvin understood the purpose of this pilgrimage. He would never walk beside the rivers of that lost and legendary world, or listen to the thunder raging above its softly rounded hills. yet one day-how far ahead?-his children's children would return to claim their heritage. The winds and the rains would scour the poisons from the burning lands and carry them to the sea, and in the depths of the sea they would waste their venom until they could harm no living things. Then the great ships that were still waiting here, on the silent, dusty plains could lift once more into space, along the road that led to home.

That was the dream: and one day, Marvin knew with a sudden flash of insight, he would pass it on to his own son, here at this same spot with the mountains behind him and the silver light from the sky streaming into his face.

He did not look back as they began the homeward journey. He could not bear to see the cold glory of the crescent Earth fade from the rocks around him, as he went to rejoin his people in their long exile.

Dog Star

When I heard Laika's frantic barking, my first reaction was one of annoyance. I turned over in my bunk and murmured sleepily, "Shut up, you silly bitch." That dreamy interlude lasted only a fraction of a second; then consciousness returned—and, with it, fear. Fear of loneliness, and fear of madness.

For a moment I dared not open my eyes; I was afraid of what I might see. Reason told me that no dog had ever set foot upon this world, that Laika was separated from me by a quarter of a million miles of space—and, far more irrevocably, five years of time.

"You've been dreaming," I told myself angrily. "Stop being a fool— open your eyes! You won't see anything except the glow of the wall paint."

That was right, of course. The tiny cabin was empty, the door tightly closed. I was alone with my memories, overwhelmed by the transcendental sadness that often comes when some bright dream fades into drab reality. The sense of loss was so desolating that I longed to return to sleep. It was well that I failed to do so, for at that moment sleep would have been death. But I did not know this for another five seconds, and during that eternity I was back on Earth, seeking what comfort I could from the past.

No one ever discovered Laika's origin, though the Observatory staff made a few enquiries and I inserted several advertisements in the Pasadena newspapers. I found her a lost and lonely ball of fluff, huddled by the roadside one summer evening when I was driving up to Palomar. Though I have never liked dogs, or indeed any animals, it was impossible to leave this helpless little creature to the mercy of the passing cars. With some qualms, wishing that I had a pair of gloves, I picked her up and dumped her in the baggage compartment. I was not going to hazard the upholstery of my new '92 Vik, and felt that she could do little damage there. In this, I was not altogether correct.

When I had parked the car at the Monastery—the astronomers' residential quarters, where I'd be living for the next week —I inspected my find without much enthusiasm. At that stage, I had intended to hand the puppy over to the janitor; but then it whimpered and opened its eyes. There was such an expression of helpless trust in them that—well, I changed my mind.

Sometimes I regretted that decision, though never for long. I had no idea how much trouble a growing dog could cause, deliberately and otherwise. My cleaning and repair bills soared; I could never be sure of finding an unravaged pair of socks or an unchewed copy of the Astrophysical Journal. But eventually Laika was both house-trained and Observatory-trained: she must have been the only dog ever to be allowed inside the two-hundred-inch dome. She would lie there quietly in the shadows for hours, while I was up in the cage making adjustments, quite content if she could hear my voice from time to time. The other astronomers became equally fond of her (it was old Dr. Anderson who suggested her name), but from the beginning she was my dog, and would obey no one else. Not that she would always obey me.

She was a beautiful animal, about ninety-five per cent Alsatian. It was that missing five per cent, I imagine, that led to her being abandoned. (I still feel a surge of anger when I think of it, but since I shall never know the facts, I may be jumping to false conclusions.) Apart from two dark patches over the eyes, most of her body was a smoky gray, and her coat was soft as silk. When her ears were pricked up, she looked incredibly intelligent and alert; sometimes I would be discussing spectral types or stellar evolution with my colleagues, and it would be hard to believe that she was not following the conversation.

Even now, I cannot understand why she became so attached to me, for I have made very few friends among human beings. Yet when I returned to the Observatory after an absence, she would go almost frantic with delight, bouncing around on her hind legs and putting her paws on my shoulders —which she could reach quite easily—all the while uttering small squeaks of joy which seemed highly inappropriate from so large a dog. I hated to leave her for more than a few days at a time, and though I could not take her with me on overseas trips, she accompanied me on most of my shorter journeys. She was with me when I drove north to attend that ill-fated seminar at Berkeley.

We were staying with university acquaintances; they had been polite about it, but obviously did not look forward to having a monster in the house. However, I assured them that Laika never gave the slightest trouble, and rather reluctantly they let her sleep in the living room. "You needn't worry about burglars tonight," I said. "We don't have any in Berkeley," they answered, rather coldly.

In the middle of the night, it seemed that they were wrong. I was awakened by a hysterical, high-pitched barking from Laika which I had heard only once before—when she had first seen a cow, and did not know what on earth to make of it. Cursing, I threw off the sheets and stumbled out into the darkness of the unfamiliar house. My main thought was to silence Laika before she roused my hosts—assuming that this was not already far too late. If there had been an intruder, he would certainly have taken flight by now. Indeed, I rather hoped that he had.

For a moment I stood beside the switch at the top of the stairs, wondering whether to throw it. Then I growled, "Shut up, Laika!" and flooded the place with light.

She was scratching frantically at the door, pausing from time to time to give that hysterical yelp. "If you want out," I said angrily, "there's no need for all that fuss." I went down, shot the bolt, and she took off into the night like a rocket.

It was very calm and still, with a waning Moon struggling to pierce the San Francisco fog. I stood in the luminous haze, looking out across the water to the lights of the city, waiting for Laika to come back so that I could chastise her suitably. I was still waiting when, for the second time in the twentieth century, the San Andreas Fault woke from its sleep.

Oddly enough, I was not frightened—at first. I can remember that two thoughts passed through my mind, in the moment before I realized the danger. Surely, I told myself, the geophysicists could have given us some warning. And then I found myself thinking, with great surprise, "I'd no idea that earthquakes make so much noise!"

It was about then that I knew that this was no ordinary quake; what happened afterward, I would prefer to forget. The Red Cross did not take me away until quite late the next morning, because I refused to leave Laika. As I looked at the shattered house containing the bodies of my friends, I knew that I owed my life to her; but the helicopter pilots could not be expected to understand that, and I cannot blame them for thinking that I was crazy, like so many of the others they had found wandering among the fires and the debris.

After that, I do not suppose we were ever apart for more than a few hours. I have been told—and I can well believe it —that I became less and less interested in human company, without being actively unsocial or misanthropic. Between them, the stars and Laika filled all my needs. We used to go for long walks together over the mountains; it was the happiest time I have ever known. There was only one flaw; I knew, though Laika could not, how soon it must end.

We had been planning the move for more than a decade. As far back as the nineteen-sixties it was realized that Earth was no place lor an astronomical observatory. Even the small pilot instruments on the Moon had far outperformed all the telescopes peering through the murk and haze of the terrestrial atmosphere. The story of Mount Wilson, Palomar, Greenwich, and the other great names was coming to an end; they would still be used for training purposes, but the research frontier must move out into space.

I had to move with it; indeed, I had already been offered the post of Deputy Director, Farside Observatory. In a few months, I could hope to solve problems I had been working on for years. Beyond the atmosphere, I would be like a blind man who had suddenly been given sight.

It was utterly impossible, of course, to take Laika with me. The only animals on the Moon were those needed for experimental purposes; it might be another generation before pets were allowed, and even then it would cost a fortune to carry them there—and to keep them alive. Providing Laika with her usual two pounds of meat a day would, I calculated, take several times my quite comfortable salary.

The choice was simple and straightforward. I could stay on Earth and abandon my career. Or I could go to the Moon— and abandon Laika.

After all, she was only a dog. In a dozen years, she would be dead, while I should be reaching the peak of my profession. No sane man would have hesitated over the matter; yet I did hesitate, and if by now you do not understand why, no further words of mine can help.

In the end, I let matters go by default. Up to the very week I was due to leave, I had still made no plans for Laika. When Dr. Anderson volunteered to look after her, I accepted numbly, with scarcely a word of thanks. The old physicist and his wife had always been fond of her, and I am afraid that they considered me indifferent and heartless—when the truth was just the opposite. We went for one more walk together over the hills; then I delivered her silently to the Andersons, and did not see her again.

Take-off was delayed almost twenty-four hours, until a major flare storm had cleared the Earth's orbit; even so, the Van Allen belts were still so active that we had to make our exit through the North Polar Gap. It was a miserable flight; apart from the usual trouble with weightlessness, we were all groggy with antiradiation drugs. The ship was already over Farside before I took much interest in the proceedings, so I missed the sight of Earth dropping below the horizon. Nor was I really sorry; I wanted no reminders, and intended to think only of the future. Yet I could not shake off that feeling of guilt; I had deserted someone who loved and trusted me, and was no better than those who had abandoned Laika when she was a puppy, beside the dusty road to Palomar.

The news that she was dead reached me a month later. There was no reason that anyone knew; the Andersons had done their best, and were very upset. She had just lost interest in living, it seemed. For a while, I think I did the same; but work is a wonderful anodyne, and my program was just getting under way. Though I never forgot Laika, in a little while the memory ceased to hurt.

Then why had it come back to haunt me, five years later, on the far side of the Moon? I was searching my mind for the reason when the metal building around me quivered as if under the impact of a heavy blow. I reacted without thinking, and was already closing the helmet of my emergency suit when the foundations slipped and the wall tore open with a short-lived scream of escaping air. Because I had automatically pressed the General Alarm button, we lost only two men, despite the fact that the tremor—the worst ever recorded on Farside—cracked all three of the Observatory's pressure domes.

It is hardly necessary for me to say that I do not believe in the supernatural; everything that happened has a perfectly rational explanation, obvious to any man with the slightest knowledge of psychology. In the second San Francisco earthquake, Laika was not the only dog to sense approaching disaster; many such cases were reported. And on Farside, my own memories must have given me that heightened awareness, when my never-sleeping subconscious detected the first faint vibrations from within the Moon.

The human mind has strange and labyrinthine ways of going about its business; it knew the signal that would most swiftly rouse me to the knowledge of danger. There is nothing more to it than that; though in a sense one could say that Laika woke me on both occasions, there is no mystery about it, no miraculous warning across the gulf that neither man nor dog can ever bridge.

Of that I am sure, if I am sure of anything. Yet sometimes I wake now, in the silence of the Moon, and wish that the dream could have lasted a few seconds longer—so that I could have looked just once more into those luminous brown eyes, brimming with an unselfish, undemanding love I have found nowhere else on this or on any other world.

Freedom of Space

Not many of you, I suppose, can imagine the time before the satellite relays gave us our present world communications system. When I was a boy, it was impossible to send TV programs across the ocean, or even to establish reliable radio contact around the curve of the Earth without picking up a fine assortment of crackles and bangs on the way. Yet now we take interference-free circuits for granted, and think nothing of seeing our friends on the other side of the globe as clearly as if we were standing face to face. Indeed, it's a simple fact that without the satellite relays, the whole structure of world commerce and industry would collapse. Unless we were up here on the space stations to bounce their messages around the globe, how do you think any of the world's big business organisations could keep their widely scattered electronic brains in touch with each other?

But all this was still in the future, back in the late seventies, when we were finishing work on the Relay Chain. I've already told you about some of our problems and near disasters; they were serious enough at the time, but in the end we overcame them all. The three stations spaced around Earth were no longer piles of girders, air cylinders, and plastic pressure chambers. Their assembly had been completed, we had moved aboard, and could now work in comfort, unhampered by space suits. And we had gravity again, now that the stations had been set slowly spinning. Not real gravity, of course; but centrifugal force feels exactly the same when you're out in space. It was pleasant being able to pour drinks and to sit down without drifting away on the first air current.

Once the three stations had been built, there was still a year's solid work to be done installing all the radio and TV equipment that would lift the world's communications networks into space. It was a great day when we established the first TV link between England and Australia. The signal was beamed up to us in Relay Two, as we sat above the center of Africa, we flashed it across to Three poised over New Guinea and they shot it down to Earth again, clear and clean after its ninety-thousand-mile journey.

These, however, were the engineers' private tests. The official opening of the system would be the biggest event in the history of world communication an elaborate global telecast, in which every nation would take part. It would be a three-hour show, as for the first time the live TV camera roamed around the world, proclaiming to mankind that the last barrier of distance was down.

The program planning, it was cynically believed, had taken as much effort as the building of the space stations in the first place, and of all the problems the planners had to solve, the most difficult was that of choosing a compare or master of ceremonies to introduce the items in the elaborate global show that would be watched by half the human race.

Heaven knows how much conniving, blackmail, and downright character assassination went on behind the scenes. All we knew was that a week before the great day, a nonscheduled rocket came up to orbit with Gregory Wendell aboard. This was quite a surprise, since Gregory wasn't as big a TV personality as, say, Jeffers Jackson in the U.S. or Vince Clifford in Britain. However, it seemed that the big boys had canceled each other out, and Gregg had got the coveted job through one of those compromises so well known to politicians.

Gregg had started his career as a disc jockey on a university radio station in the American Midwest, and had worked his way up through the Hollywood and Manhattan night club circuits until he had a daily, nation-wide program of his own. Apart from his cynical yet relaxed personality, his biggest asset was his deep velvet voice, for which he could probably thank his Negro blood. Even when you flatly disagreed with what he was saying even, indeed, when he was tearing you to pieces in an interview it was still a pleasure to listen to him.

We gave him the grand tour of the space station, and even (strictly against regulations) took him out through the air lock in a space suit. He loved it all, but there were two things he liked in particular.

"This air you make," he said, "it beats the stuff eve to breathe down in New York. This is the first time my sinus trouble has gone since I went into TV." He also relished the low gravity; at the station's rim, a man had half his normal, Earth weight and at the axis he had no weight at all.

However, the novelty of his sww~di~ didn't distract Gregg from his job. He spent hours at Communications Central, polishing his script and getting his cues right, and studying the dozens of monitor screens that would be his windows on the world. I came across him once while he was running through his introduction of Queen Elizabeth, who would be speaking from Buckingham Palace at the very end of the program. He was so intent on his rehearsal that he never even noticed I was standing beside him.

Well, that telecast is now part of history. For the first time a billion human beings watched a single program that came "Eve" from every corner of the Earth, and was a roll call of the world's greatest citizens. Hundreds of cameras on land and sea and air looked inquiringly at the turning globe; and at the end there was that wonderful shot of the Earth through a zoom lens on the space station, making the whole planet recede until it was lost among the stars....

There were a few hitches, of course. One camera on the bed of the Atlantic wasn't ready on cue, and we had to spend some extra time looking at the Taj Mahal. And owing to a switching error Russian subtitles were superimposed on the South American transmissions, while half the USSR found itself trying to read Spanish. But this was nothing to what might have happened.

Through the entire three hours, introducing the famous and the unknown with equal ease, came the mellow yet never orotund flow of Gregg's voice. He did a magnificent job; the congratulations came pouring up the beam the moment the broadcast finished.

But he didn't hear them; he made one short, private call to his agent, and then went to bed. Next morning, the Earth-bound ferry was waiting to take him back to any job he cared to accept.

But it left without Gregg Wendell, now junior station announcer of Relay Two.

"They'll think I'm crazy," he said, beaming happily, "but why should I go back to that rat race down there? I've all the universe to look at, I can breathe smog-free air, the low gravity makes me feel a Hercules, and my three darling ex wives can't get at me." He kissed his hand to the departing rocket.

"So long, Earth," he called.

"I'll be back when I start pining for Broadway traffic jams and bleary penthouse dawns. And if I get homesick, I can look at anywhere on the planet just by turning a switch. Why, I'm more in the middle of things here than I could ever be on Earth, yet I can cut myself off from the human race whenever I want to."

He was still smiling as he watched the ferry begin the long fall backto Earth, toward the fame and fortune that could have been his. Andthen, whistling cheerfully, he left the observation lounge in eight-foot strides to read the weather forecast for Lower Patagonia.

Passer-by

It's only fair to warn you, right at the start, that this is a story with no ending. But it has a definite beginning, for it was while we were both students at Astrotech that I met Julie. She was in her final year of solar physics when I was graduating, and during our last year at college we saw a good deal of each other. I've still got the woollen tamo'shanter she knitted so that I wouldn't bump my head against my space helmet. (No, I never had the nerve to wear it.) Unfortunately, when I was assigned to Satellite Two Julie went to the Solar Observatory at the same distance from Earth, but a couple of degrees eastward along the orbit. So there we were, sitting twenty-two thousand miles above the middle of Africa but with nine hundred miles of empty, hostile space between us.

At first we were both so busy that the pang of separation was somewhat lessened. But when the novelty of life in space had worn off, our thoughts began to bridge the gulf that divided us. And not only our thoughts, for I'd made friends with the communications people, and we used to have little chats over the intersection TV circuit. In some ways it made matters worse seeing each other face to face and never knowing just how many other people were looking in at the same time.

There's not much privacy in a space station.... Sometimes I'd focus one of our telescopes onto the distant, brilliant star of the observatory.

In the crystal clarity of space, I could use enormous magnifications, and could see every detail of our neighbors' equipment the solar telescopes, the pressurized spheres of the living quarters that housed the staff, the slim pencils of visiting ferry rockets that had climbed up from Earth. Very often there would be space-suited figures moving among the maze of apparatus, and I would strain my eyes in a hopeless attempt at identification. It's hard enough to recognize anyone in a space suit when you're only a few feet apart but that didn't stop me from trying.

We'd resigned ourselves to waiting, with what patience we could muster, until our Earth leave was due in six months' time, when we had an unexpected stroke of luck. Less than half our tour of duty had passed when the head of the transport section suddenly announced that he was going outside with a butterfly net to catch meteors. He didn't become violent, but had to be shipped hastily back to Earth. I took over his job on a temporary basis and now had in theory at least the freedom of space.

There were ten of the little low-powered rocket scooters under my proud command, as well as four of the larger inter station shuttles used to ferry stores and personnel from orbit to orbit. I couldn't hope to borrow one of those, but after several weeks of careful organising I was able to carry out the plan I'd conceived some two microseconds after being told I was now head of transport.

There's no need to tell how I juggled duty lists, cooked logs and fuel registers, and persuaded my colleagues to cover up for me. All that matters is that, about once a week, I would climb into my personal space suit, strap myself to the spidery framework of a Mark III Scooter, and drift away from the station at minimum power. When I was well clear, I'd go over to full throttle, and the tiny rocket motor would hustle me across the nine-hundred-mile gap to the observatory.

The trip took about thirty minutes, and the navigational requirements were elementary. I could see where I was going and where I'd come from, yet I don't mind admitting that I often felt well, a trifle lonely around the mid-point of the journey. There was no other solid matter within almost five hundred miles and it looked an awfully long way down to Earth. It was a great help, at such moments, to tune the suit radio to the general service band, and to listen to all the back-chat between ships and stations.

At mid-flight I'd have to spin the scooter around and start braking, and ten minutes later the observatory would be close enough for its details to be visible to the unaided eye. Very shortly after that I'd drift up to a small, plastic pressure bubble that was in the process of being fitted out as a spectroscopic laboratory and there would be Julie, waiting on the other side of the air lock.... I won't pretend that we confined our discussions to the latest results in astrophysics, or the progress of the satellite construction schedule. Few things, indeed, were further from our thoughts; and the journey home always seemed to flash by at a quite astonishing speed.

It was around mid-orbit on one of those homeward trips that the radar started to flash on my little control panel. There was something large at extreme range, and it was coming in fast. A meteor, I told myself maybe even a small asteroid. Anything giving such a signal should be visible to the eye: I read off the bearings and searched the star fields in the indicated direction.

The thought of a collision never even crossed my mind; space is so inconceivably vast that I was thousands of times safer than a man crossing a busy street on Earth.

There it was a bright and steadily growing star near the foot of Orion. It already outshone Rigel, and seconds later it was not merely a star, but had begun to show a visible disk. Now it was moving as fast as I could turn my head; it grew to a tiny, misshaped moon, then dwindled and shrank with the same silent, inexorable speed.

I suppose I had a clear view of it for perhaps half a second, and that half-second has haunted me all my life. The object had already vanished by the time I thought of checking the radar again, so I had no way of gauging how close it came, and hence how large it really was. It could have been a small object a hundred feet away or a very large one, ten miles off. There is no sense of perspective in space, and unless you know what you are looking at, you cannot judge its distance.

Of course, it could have been a very large and oddly shaped meteor; I can never be sure that my eyes, straining to grasp the details of so swiftly moving an object, were not hopelessly deceived. I may have imagined that I saw that broken, crumpled prow, and the cluster of dark ports like the sightless sockets of a skull. Of one thing only was I certain, even in that brief and fragmentary vision. If it was a ship, it was not one of ours. Its shape was utterly alien, and it was very, very old.

It may be that the greatest discovery of all time slipped from my grasp as I struggled with my thoughts midway between the two space stations.

But I had no measurements of speed or direction; whatever it was that I had glimpsed was now lost beyond recapture in the wastes of the solar system. What should I have done? No one would ever have believed me, for I would have had no proof. Had I made a report, there would have been endless trouble. I should have become the laughingstock of the Space Service, would have been reprimanded for misuse of equipment and would certainly not have been able to see Julie again. And to me, at that age, nothing else was as important. If you've been in love yourself, you'll understand; if not, then no explanation is any use. So I said nothing. To some other man (how many centuries hence?) will go the fame for proving that we were not the first-born of the children of the sun. Whatever it may be that is circling out there on its eternal orbit can wait, as it has waited ages already. Yet I sometimes wonder. Would I have made a report, after all had I known that Julie was going to marry someone else?

The Call of the Stars

Down there on Earth the twentieth century is dying. As I look across at the shadowed globe blocking the stars, I can see the lights of a hundred sleepless cities, and there are moments when I wish that I could be among the crowds now surging and singing in the streets of London, Capetown, Rome, Paris, Berlin, Madrid. . . . Yes, I can see them all at a single glance, burning like fireflies against the darkened planet. The line of midnight is now bisecting Europe: in the eastern Mediterranean a tiny, brilliant star is pulsing as some exuberant pleasure ship waves her searchlights to the sky. I think she is deliberately aiming at us; for the past few minutes the flashes have been quite regular and startlingly bright. Presently I'll call the communications center and find out who she is, so that I can radio back our own greetings.

Passing into history now, receding forever down the stream of time, is the most incredible hundred years the world has ever seen. It opened with the conquest of the air, saw at its mid-point the unlocking of the atom—and now ends with the bridging of space.

(For the past five minutes I've been wondering what's happening to Nairobi; now I realize that they are putting on a mammoth fireworks display. Chemically fueled rockets may be obsolete out here—but they're still using lots of them down on Earth tonight.)

The end of a century—and the end of a millennium. What will the hundred years that begin with two and zero bring? The planets, of course; floating there in space, only a mile away, are the ships of the first Martian expedition. For two years I have watched them grow, assembled piece by piece, as the space station itself was built by the men I worked with a generation ago.

Those ten ships are ready now, with all their crews aboard, waiting for the final instrument check and the signal for departure. Before the first day of the new century has passed its noon, they will be tearing free from the reins of Earth, to head out toward the strange world that may one day be man's second home.

As I look at the brave little fleet that is now preparing to challenge infinity, my mind goes back forty years, to the days when the first satellites were launched and the Moon still seemed very far away. And I remember—indeed, I have never forgotten—my father's fight to keep me down on Earth.

There were not many weapons he had failed to use. Ridicule had been the first: "Of course they can do it," he had sneered, "but what's the point? Who wants to go out into space while there's so much to be done here on Earth? There's not a single planet in the Solar System where men can live. The Moon's a burnt-out slag heap, and everywhere else is even worse. This is where we were meant to live."

Even then (I must have been eighteen or so at the time) I could tangle him up in points of logic. I can remember answering, "How do you know where we were meant to live, Dad? After all, we were in the sea for about a billion years before we decided to tackle the land. Now we're making the next big jump: I don't know where it will lead—nor did that first fish when it crawled up on the beach, and started to sniff the air."

So when he couldn't outargue me, he had tried subtler pressures. He was always talking about the dangers of space travel, and the short working life of anyone foolish enough to get involved in rocketry. At that time, people were still scared of meteors and cosmic rays; like the "Here Be Dragons" of the old map makers, they were the mythical monsters on the still-blank celestial charts. But they didn't worry me; if anything, they added the spice of danger to my dreams.

While I was going through college, Father was comparatively quiet. My training would be valuable whatever profession I took up in later life, so he could not complain— though he occasionally grumbled about the money I wasted buying all the books and magazines on astronautics that I could find. My college record was good, which naturally pleased him; perhaps he did not realize that it would also help me to get my way.

All through my final year I had avoided talking of my plans. I had even given the impression (though I am sorry for that now) that I had abandoned my dream of going into space. Without saying anything to him, I put in my application to Astrotech, and was accepted as soon as I had graduated.

The storm broke when that long blue envelope with the embossed heading "Institute of Astronautical Technology" dropped into the mailbox. I was accused of deceit and ingratitude, and I do not think I ever forgave my father for destroying the pleasure I should have felt at being chosen for the most exclusive—and most glamorous—apprenticeship the world has ever known.

The vacations were an ordeal; had it not been for Mother's sake, I do not think I would have gone home more than once a year, and I always left again as quickly as I could. I had hoped that Father would mellow as my training progressed and as he accepted the inevitable, but he never did.

Then had come that stiff and awkward parting at the spaceport, with the rain streaming down from leaden skies and beating against the smooth walls of the ship that seemed so eagerly waiting to climb into the eternal sunlight beyond the reach of storms. I know now what it cost my father to watch the machine he hated swallow up his only son: for I understand many things today that were hidden from me then.

He knew, even as we parted at the ship, that he would never see me again. Yet his old, stubborn pride kept him from saying the only words that might have held me back. I knew that he was ill, but how ill, he had told no one. That was the only weapon he had not used against me, and I respect him for it.

Would I have stayed had I known? It is even more futile to speculate about the unchangeable past than the unforeseeable future; all I can say now is that I am glad I never had to make the choice. At the end he let me go; he gave up his fight against my ambition, and a little while later his fight with Death.

So I said good-by to Earth, and to the father who loved me but knew no way to say it. He lies down there on the planet I can cover with my hand; how strange it is to think that of the countless billion human beings whose blood runs in my veins, I was the very first to leave his native world. . . .

The new day is breaking over Asia; a hairline of fire is rimming the eastern edge of Earth. Soon it will grow into a burning crescent as the sun comes up out of the Pacific—yet Europe is preparing for sleep, except for those revelers who will stay up to greet the dawn.

And now, over there by the flagship, the ferry rocket is coming back for the last visitors from the station. Here comes the message I have been waiting for: CAPTAIN STEVENS PRESENTS HIS COMPLIMENTS TO THE STATION COMMANDER. BLAST-OFF WILL BE IN NINETY MINUTES; HE WILL BE GLAD TO SEE YOU ABOARD NOW.

Well, Father, now I know how you felt: time has gone full circle. Yet I hope that I have learned from the mistakes we both made, long ago. I shall remember you when I go over there to the flagship Starfire and say good-by to the grandson you never knew.

The Next Tenants

"The number of mad scientists who wish to conquer the world," said Harry Purvis, looking thoughtfully at his beer, "has been grossly exaggerated. In fact, I can remember encountering only a single one."

"Then there couldn't have been many others," commented Bill Temple, a little acidly. "It's not the sort of thing one would be likely to forget."

"I suppose not," replied Harry, with that air of irrefragable innocence which is so disconcerting to his critics. "And, as a matter of fact, this scientist wasn't really mad. There was no doubt, though, that he was out to conquer the world. Or if you want to be really precise-to let the world be conquered."

"And by whom?" asked George Whitley. "The Martians? Or the well-known little green men from Venus?"

"Neither of them. He was collaborating with someone a lot nearer home. You'll realize who I mean when I tell you he was a myrmecologist."

"A which-what?" asked George.

"Let him get on with the story," said Drew, from the other side of the bar. "It's past ten, and if I can't get you all out by closing time this week, I'll lose my license."

"Thank you," said Harry with dignity, handing over his glass for a refill. "This all happened about two years ago, when I was on a mission in the Pacific. It was rather hush-hush, but in view of what's happened since there's no harm in talking about it. Three of us scientists were landed on a certain Pacific atoll not a thousand miles fromBikini , and given a week to set up some detection equipment.it was intended, of course, to keep an eye on our good friends and allies when they started playing with thermo-nuclear reactions to pick some crumbs from the A.E.C.'s table, as it were. The Russians, naturally, were doing the same thing, and occasionally we ran into each other and then both sides would pretend that there was nobody here but us chickens.

"What!" gasped everybody.

"-several hundred millions," continued Purvis calmly, "of which number, one was human. I came across him when I went inland one day to have a look at the scenery."

"Inland?" asked George Whitley. "I thought you said it was an atoll. How can a ring of coral-"

"It was a very plump atoll," said Harry firmly. "Anyway, who's telling this story?" He waited defiantly for a moment until he had the right of way again.

"Here I was, then, walking up a charming little river-course underneath the coconut palms, when to my great surprise I came across a waterwheel-a very modem-looking one, driving a dynamo. If I'd been sensible, I suppose I'd have gone back and told my companions, but I couldn't resist the challenge and decided to do some reconnoitering on my own.' I remembered that there were still supposed to be Japanese troops around who didn't know that the war was over, but that explanation seemed a bit unlikely.

"I followed the power-line up a hill, and there on the other side was a low, whitewashed building set in a large clearing. All over this clearing were tall, irregular mounds of earth, linked together with a network of wires. It was one of the most baffling sights I have ever seen, and I stood and stared for a good ten minutes, trying to decide what was going on. The longer I looked, the less sense it seemed to make.

I was debating what to do when a tall, white-haired man came out of the building and walked over to one of the mounds. He was carrying some kind of apparatus and had a pair of earphones slung around his neck, so I guessed that he was using a Geiger counter. It was just about then that I realized what those tall mounds were. They were termitaries . . . the skyscrapers, in comparison to their makers, far taller than the Empire State Building , in which the so-called white ants live.

"I watched with great interest, but complete bafflement, while the elderly scientist inserted his apparatus into the base of the termitary , listened intently for a moment, and then walked back towards the building. By this time I was so curious that I decided to make my presence known. Whatever research was going on here obviously had nothing to do with international politics, so I was the only one who'd have anything to hide. You'll appreciate later just what a miscalculation that was.

"I yelled for attention and walked down the hill, waving my arms. The stranger halted and watched me approaching: he didn't look particularly surprised. As I came closer I saw that he had a straggling moustache that gave him a faintly Oriental appearance. He was about sixty years old, and carried himself very erect. Though he was wearing nothing but a pair of shorts, he looked so dignified that I felt rather ashamed of my noisy approach.

"'Good morning, I said apologetically. 'I didn't know that there was anyone else on this island. I'm with an- er-scientific survey party over on the other side.'

"At this, the stranger's eyes lit up. 'Ah,' he said, in almost perfect English, 'a fellow scientist! I'm very pleased to meet you. Come into the house.

"I introduced myself first, and as I'd hoped he promptly responded. He was one Professor Taka to, a biologist from a leading Japanese university. He didn't look particularly Japanese, apart from the moustache I've mentioned. With his erect, dignified bearing he reminded me more of an old Kentucky colonel I once knew.

"After he'd given me some unfamiliar but refreshing Wine, we sat and talked for a couple of hours. Like most scientists he seemed happy to meet someone who would appreciate his work. It was true that my interests lay in physics and chemistry rather than on the biological side, but I found Professor Takato's research quite fascinating.

"I don't suppose you know much about termites, so It remind you of the salient facts. They're among the most highly evolved of the social insects, and live in vast colonies throughout the tropics. They can't stand cold weather, nor, oddly enough, can they endure direct sunlight. When they have to get from one place to another, they construct little covered roadways. They seem to have some unknown and almost instantaneous means of communication, and though the individual termites are pretty helpless and dumb, a whole colony behaves like an intelligent animal. Some writers have drawn comparisons between a termitary and a human body, which is also composed of individual living cells making up an entity much higher than the basic units. The termites are often called 'white ants', but that's a completely incorrect name as they aren't ants at all but quite a different species of insect. Or should I say 'genus'? I'm pretty vague about this sort of thing . . . .

"Excuse this little lecture, but after I'd listened to Takato for a while I began to get quite enthusiastic about termites myself. Did you know, for example, that they not only cultivate gardens but also keep cows-insect cows, of course-and milk them? Yes, they're sophisticated little devils, even though they do it all by instinct.

"But I'd better tell you something about the Professor. Although he was alone at the moment, and had lived on the island for several years, he had a number of assistants who brought equipment from Japan and helped him in his work. His first great achievement was to do for the termites what von Frische had done with bees-he'd learned their language. It was much more complex than the system of communication that bees use, which as you probably know, is based on dancing. I understood that the network of wires linking the termitaries to the lab not only enabled Professor Takato to listen to the termites talking among each other, but also permitted him to speak to them. That's not really as fantastic as it sounds, if you use the word "speak" in its widest sense, We speak to a good many animals-not always with our voices, by any means. When you throw a stick for your dog and expect him to run and fetch it, that's a form of speech-sign language. The Professor, I gathered, had worked out some kind of code which the termites understood, though how efficient it was at communicating ideas I didn't know.

"I came back each day, when I could spare the time, and by the end of the week we were firm friends. It may surprise you that I was able to conceal these visits from my colleagues, but the island was quite large and we each did a lot of exploring. I felt somehow that Professor Takato was my private property, and did not wish to expose him to the curiosity of my companions. They were rather uncouth characters-graduates of some provincial university like Oxford or Cambridge.

"I'm glad to say that I was able to give the Professor a certain amount of assistance, fixing his radio and lining up some of his electronic gear. He used radioactive tracers a good deal, to follow individual termites around. He'd been tracking one with a Geiger counter when I first met him, in fact.

"'I think,' he said softly, 'thatyou physicists are playing with your toys again.And very big ones, this time.'

"'I'm afraid you're right,' I answered. We wouldn't be sure until the readings had been analyzed, but it looked as if Teller and his team had started the hydrogen reaction. 'Before long, we'll.be able to make the first A-bombs look like damp squibs.'

"'My family,' said Professor Takato , without any emotion, 'was at Nagasaki.'

"There wasn't a great deal I could say to that, and I was glad when he went on to add: 'Have you ever wondered who will take over when we are finished?'

"'Your termites?I said, half facetiously. He seemed to hesitate for a moment. Then he said quietly, 'Come with me; I have not shown you everything.'

"We walked over to a comer of the lab where some equipment lay concealed beneath dust-sheets, and the Professor uncovered a rather curious piece of apparatus. At first sight it looked like one of the manipulators used for the remote handling of dangerously radioactive materials. There were handgrips that conveyed movements through rods and levers, but everything seemed to focus on a small box a few inches on a side. 'What is it? I asked.

"'It's a micromanipulator. The French developed them for biological work. There aren't many around yet.'

"Then I remembered. These were devices with which, by the use of suitable reduction gearing, one could carry out the most incredibly delicate operations. You moved your finger an inch-and the tool you were controlling moved a thousandth of an inch. The French scientists who had developed this technique had built tiny forges on which they could construct minute scalpels and tweezers from fused glass. Working entirely through microscopes, they had been able to dissect individual cells. Removing an appendix from a termite (in the highly doubtful event of the insect possessing one) would be child's play with such an instrument.

"'I am not very skilled at using the manipulator,' confessed Takato. ' One of my assistants does all the work with it. I have shown no one else this, but you have been very helpful Come with me, please.'

"We went out into the open, and walked past the avenues of tall, cement-hard mounds. They were not all of the same architectural design, for there are many different kinds of termites-some, indeed, don't build mounds at all. I felt rather like a giant walking through Manhattan, for these were skyscrapers, each with its own teeming population.

"There was a small metal (not wooden-the termites would soon have fixed that!)hut beside one of the mounds, and as we entered it the glare of sunlight was banished. The Professor threw a switch, and a faint red glow enabled me to see various types of optical equipment.

"'Of course,' I said. 'Snipers had them fixed on their rifles so that they could go sharp-shooting in the dark. Very ingenious things -I'm glad you've found a civilized use for them.'

"It was a long time before Professor Takato found what he wanted. He seemed to be steering some kind of periscope arrangement,

---

71

probing through the corridors of the termite city. Then he said: 'Quick-before they've gone!'

"I moved over and took his position. It was a second or so before my eye focused properly, and longer still before I understood the scale of the picture I was seeing. Then I saw six termites, greatly enlarged, moving rather rapidly across the field of vision. They were traveling in a group, like the huskies forming a dog-team. And that was a very good analogy, because they were towing a sledge . . . .

"I was so astonished that I never even noticed what kind of load they were moving. When they had vanished from sight, I turned to Professor Takato . My eyes had now grown accustomed to the faint red glow, and I could see him quite well.

"'So that's the sort of tool you've been building with your micromanipulator!'I said. 'It's amazing-I'd never have believed it.'

"'But that is nothing,' replied the Professor. 'Performing fleas will pull a cart around. I haven't told you what is so important. We only made a few of those sledges. The one you saw they constructed themselves.'

"He let that sink in: it took some time. Then he continued quietly, but with a kind of controlled enthusiasm in his voice: Remember that the termites, as individuals, have virtually no intelligence. But the colony as a whole is a very high type of organism -and an immortal one, barring accidents. It froze in its present instinctive pattern millions of years before Man was born, and by itself it can never escape from its present sterile perfection. It has reached a dead-end-because it has no tools, no effective way of controlling nature. I have given it the lever, to increase its power, and now the sledge, to improve its efficiency. I have thought of the wheel, but it is best to let that wait for a later stage-it would not be very useful now. The results have exceeded my expectations. I started with this termitary alone-but now they all have the same tools. They have taught each other, and that proves they can cooperate. True, they have wars-but not when there is enough food for all, as there is here.

"'But you cannot judge the termitary by human standards. What I hope to do is to jolt its rigid, frozen culture-to knock it out of the groove in which it has stuck for so many millions of years. I will give it more tools, more new techniques-and before I die, I hope to see it beginning to invent things for itself.'

"'Why are you doing this?I asked, for I knew there was more than mere scientific curiosity here.

"'Because I do not believe that Man will survive, yet I hope to preserve some of the things he has discovered. If he is to be a dead-end, I think that another race should be given a helping hand. Do you know why I chose this island? It was so that my experiment should remain isolated. My super termite, if it ever evolves, will have to remain here until it has reached a very high level of attainment.Until it can cross the Pacific, in fact . . . .

"I could think of nothing to say: this glimpse of the Professor's dreams was so overwhelming-and yet, in view of what I had just seen, so convincing.For I knew that Professor Takato was not mad. He was a visionary, and there was a sublime detachment about his outlook, but it was based on a secure foundation of scientific achievement.

"And it was not that he was hostile to mankind: he was sorry for it. He simply believed that humanity had shot its bolt, and wished to save something from the wreckage. I could not feel it in my heart to blame him.

"We must have been in that little hut for a long time, exploring possible futures. I remember suggesting that perhaps there might be some kind of mutual understanding, since two culturesso utterly dissimilar as Man and Termite need have no cause for conflict. But I couldn't really believe this, and if a contest comes, I'm not certain who will win. For what use would man's weapons be against an intelligent enemy who couldlay waste all the wheat fields and all the rice crops in the world?

"When we came out into the open once more, it was almostdusk . It was then that the Professor made his final revelation.

"'In a few weeks,' he said, 'I am going to take the biggest step of all.'

"'And what is that? I asked.

"'Cannot you guess? I am going to give them fire.'

"Those words did something to my spine. I felt a chill that had nothing to do with the oncoming night. The glorious sunset that was taking place beyond the palms seemed symbolic-and suddenly I realized that the symbolism was even deeper than I had thought.

"That sunset was one of the most beautiful I had ever seen, and it was partly of man's making. Up there in the stratosphere, the dust of an island that had died this day was encircling the earth. My race had taken a great step forward; but did it matter now?

"'I am going to give them fire.' Somehow, I never doubted that the Professor would succeed. And when he had done so, the forces that my own race had just unleashed would not save it . . . .

"The flying boat came to collect us the next day, and I did not see Takato again. He is still there, and I think he is the most important man in the world. While our politicians wrangle, he is making us obsolete.

"Do you think that someone ought to stop him? There may still be time. I've often thought about it, but I've never been able to think of a really convincing reason why I should interfere. Once or twice I nearly made up my mind, but then I'd pick up the newspaper and see the headlines.

"I think we should let them have the chance. I don't see how they could make a worse job of it than we've done."

OUT OF THE SUN

Arthur C. Clarke is a true citizen of the world. Where he is at any given moment only his travel agent is likely to know: perhaps in New York conferring with his publishers, perhaps excavating sunken treasure off the coast of Ceylon, perhaps supervising the filming of a movie in London, perhaps studying the cored formations of Australia's Great Barrier Reef, perhaps watching a rocket blasting moonward from Cape Kennedy. He was born in England, but he is at home on any continent, and probably will be found sightseeing on Mars and Venus as soon as commercial service to those ports of call is inaugurated.

As an acknowledged master of science fiction, Clarke's presence in any anthology is almost mandatory. He works within the great tradition of H. G. Wells, combining literary artistry with scientific accuracy to create stories of stirring wonder and breathtaking provocativeness. Here Clarke offers a fitting epilogue for this collection of stories of alien life: a glimpse of a life-form so incredibly strange that we poor mortals can barely begin to comprehend its nature.

If you have only lived on Earth, you have never seen the sun. Of course, we could not look at it directly, but only through dense filters that cut its rays down to endurable brilliance. It hung there forever above the low, jagged hills to the west of the Observatory, neither rising nor setting, yet moving around a small circle in the sky during the eighty-eight-day year of our little world. For it is not quite true to say that Mercury keeps the same face always turned toward the sun; it wobbles slightly on its axis, and there is a narrow twilight belt which knows such terrestrial commonplaces as dawn and sunset.

We were on the edge of the twilight zone, so that we could take advantage of the cool shadows yet could keep the sun under continuous surveillance as it hovered there above the hills. It was a full-time job for fifty astronomers and other assorted scientists; when we've kept it up for a hundred years or so, we may know something about the small star that brought life to Earth.

There wasn't a single band of solar radiation that someone at the Observatory had not made a life's study and was watching like a hawk. From the far X-rays to the longest of radio waves, we had set our traps and snares; as soon as the sun thought of something new, we were ready for it. So we imagined...

The sun's flaming heart beats in a slow, eleven-year rhythm, and we were near the peak of the cycle. Two of the greatest spots ever recorded-each of them large enough to swallow a hundred Earths-had drifted across the disk like great black funnels piercing deeply into the turbulent outer layers of the sun. They were black, of course, only by contrast with the brilliance all around them; even their dark, cool cores were hotter and brighter than an electric arc. We had just watched the second of them disappear around the edge of the disk, wondering if it would survive to reappear two weeks later, when something blew up on the equator.

It was not too spectacular at first, partly because it was almost exactly beneath us-at the precise center of the sun's disk-and so was merged into all the activity around it. If it had been near the edge of the sun, and thus projected against the background of space, it would have been truly awe-inspiring.

Imagine the simultaneous explosion of a million H-bombs. You can't? Nor can anyone else-but that was the sort of thing we were watching climb up toward us at hundreds of miles a second, straight out of the sun's spinning equator. At first it formed a narrow jet, but it was quickly frayed around the edges by the magnetic and gravitational forces that were fighting against it. The central core kept right on, and it was soon obvious that it had escaped from the sun completely and was headed out into space-with us as its first target.

Though this had happened half a dozen times before, it was always exciting. It meant that we could capture some of the very substance of the sun as it went hurtling past in a great cloud of electrified gas.

There was no danger; by the tune it reached us it would be far too tenuous to do any damage, and, indeed, it would take sensitive instruments to detect it at all.

One of those instruments was the Observatory's radar, which was in continual use to map the invisible ionized layers that surround the sun for millions of miles. This was my department; as soon as there was any hope of picking up the oncoming cloud against the solar background, I aimed my giant radio mirror toward it.

It came in sharp and clear on the long-range screen-a vast, luminous island still moving outward from the sun at hundreds of miles a second. At this distance it was impossible to see its finer details, for my radar waves were taking minutes to make the round trip and to bring me back the information they were presenting on the screen. Even at its speed of not far short of a million miles an hour, it would be almost two days before the escaping prominence reached the orbit of Mercury and swept past us toward the outer planets. But neither Venus nor Earth would record its passing, for they were nowhere near its line of flight.

The hours drifted by; the sun had settled down after the immense convulsions that had shot so many millions of tons of its substance into space, never to return. The aftermath of that eruption was now a slowly twisting and turning cloud a hundred times the size of Earth, and soon it would be close enough for the short-range radar to reveal its finer structure.

Despite all the years I have been in the business, it still gives me a thrill to watch that line of light paint its picture on the screen as its spins in synchronism with the narrow beam of radio waves from the transmitter. I sometimes think of myself as a blind man exploring the space around him with a stick that may be a hundred million miles in length. For man is truly blind to the things I study; these great clouds of ionized gas moving far out from the sun are completely invisible to the eye and even to the most sensitive of photographic plates. They are ghosts that briefly haunt the solar system during the few hours of their existence; if they did not reflect our radar waves or disturb our magnetometers, we should never know that they were there.

The picture on the screen looked not unlike a photograph of a spiral nebula, for as the cloud slowly rotated it trailed ragged arms of gas for ten thousand miles around it. Or it might have been a terrestrial hurricane that I was watching from above as it spun through the atmosphere of Earth. The internal structure was extremely complicated and was changing minute by minute beneath the action of forces which we have never fully understood. Rivers of fire were flowing in curious paths under what could only be the influence of electric fields; but why were they appearing from nowhere and disappearing again as if matter was being created and destroyed? And what were those gleaming nodules, larger than the moon, that were being swept along like boulders before a flood?

Now it was less than a million miles away; it would be upon us in little more than an hour. The automatic cameras were recording every complete sweep of the radar scan, storing up evidence which was to keep us arguing for years. The magnetic disturbance riding ahead of the cloud had already reached us; indeed, there was hardly an instrument in the Observatory that was not reacting in some way to the onrushing apparition.

I switched to the short-range scanner, and the image of the cloud expanded so enormously that only its central portion was on the screen. At the same time I began to change frequency, turning across the spectrum to differentiate among~ the various levels. The shorter the wave length, the farther you can penetrate into a layer of ionized gas; by this technique I hope to get a kind of X-ray picture of the cloud's interior.

It seemed to change before my eyes as I sliced down through the tenuous outer envelope with its trailing arms -and approached the denser core. "Denser," of course, was a purely relative word; by terrestrial standards even its most closely packed regions were still a fairly good vacuum. I had almost reached the limit of my frequency band, and could shorten the wave length no farmer, when I noticed the curious, tight little echo not far from the center of the screen.

It was oval and much more sharp-edged than the knots of gas" we had watched adrift in the cloud's fiery streams. Even in that first glimpse, I knew that here was something very strange and outside all previous records of solar phenomena. I watched it for a dozen scans of the radar beam, then called my assistant away from the radiospectrograph, with which he was analyzing the velocities of the swirling gas as it spun toward us.

"Look, Don," I asked him, "have you ever seen anything like that?"

"No," he answered after a careful examination. "What holds it together? It hasn't changed its shape for the last two minutes."

"That's what puzzles me. Whatever it is, it should have started to break up by now, with all that disturbance going on around it. But it seems as stable as ever."

"How big would you say it is?"

I switched on the calibration grid and took a quick reading.

"It's about five hundred miles long, and half that in width."

"Is this the largest picture you can get?"

"I'm afraid so. We'll have to wait until it's closer before we can see what makes it tick."

Don gave a nervous little laugh.

"This is crazy," he said, "but do you know something? I feel as if I'm looking at an amoeba under a microscope."

I did not answer; for, with what I can only describe as a sensation of intellectual vertigo, exactly the same thought had entered my mind.

We forgot about the rest of the cloud, but luckily the automatic cameras kept up their work, and no important observations were lost. From now on we had eyes only for that sharp-edged lens of gas that was growing minute by minute as it raced toward us. When it was no farther away than is the moon from Earth, it began to show the first signs of its internal structure, revealing a curious mottled appearance that was never quite the same on two successive sweeps of the scanner.

By now, half the Observatory staff had joined us in the radar room, yet there was complete silence as the oncoming enigma grew swiftly across the screen. It was coming straight toward us; in a few minutes it would hit Mercury somewhere in the center of the daylight side, and that would be the end of it-whatever it was. From the moment we obtained our first really detailed view until the screen became blank again could not have been more than five minutes; for every one of us, that five minutes will haunt us all our lives.

We were looking at what seemed to be a translucent oval, its interior laced with a network of almost invisible lines. Where the lines crossed, there appeared to be tiny, pulsing nodes of light; we could never be quite sure of their existence because the radar took almost a minute to paint the complete picture on the screen-and between each sweep the object moved several thousand miles. There was no doubt, however, that the network itself existed; the cameras settled any arguments about that.

So strong was the impression that we were looking at a solid object that I took a few moments off from the radar screen and hastily focused one of the optical telescopes on the sky. Of course, there was nothing to be seen-no sign of anything silhouetted against the sun's pock-marked disk. This was a case where vision failed completely and only the electrical senses of the radar were of any use. The thing that was coming toward us out of the sun was as transparent as air-and far more tenuous.

As those last moments ebbed away, I am quite sure that every one of us had reached the same conclusion-and was waiting for someone to say it first. What we were seeing was impossible, yet the evidence was there before our eyes. We were looking at life, where no life could exist...

The eruption had hurled the thing out of its normal environment, deep down in the flaming atmosphere of the sun. It was a miracle that it had survived its journey through space; already it must be dying, as the forces that controlled its huge, invisible body lost their hold over the electrified gas which was the only substance it possessed.

Today, now that I have run through those films a hundred times, the idea no longer seems so strange to me. For what is life-but organized energy? Does it matter what form that energy takes-whether it is chemical, as we know it on Earth, or •purely electrical, as it seemed to be here? Only the pattern is important; the substance itself is of no significance. But at the time I did not think of this; I was conscious only of a vast and overwhelming wonder as I watched this creature of the sun live out the final moments of its existence.

Was it intelligent? Could it understand the strange doom that had befallen it? There are a thousand such questions that may never be answered. It is hard to see how a creature born in the fires of the sun itself could know anything of the external universe, or could even sense the existence of something as unutterably cold as rigid nongaseous matter. The living island that was falling upon us from space could never have conceived, however intelligent it might be, of the world it was so swiftly approaching.

Now it filled our sky-and perhaps, in those last few seconds, it knew that something strange was ahead of it. It may have sensed the far-flung magnetic field of Mercury or felt the tug of our little world's gravitational pull. For it had begun to change; the luminous lines that must have been what passed for its nervous system were clumping together in new patterns, and I would have given much to know their meaning. It may be that I was looking into the brain of a mindless beast in its last convulsion of fear-or of a godlike being making its peace with the universe.

Then the radar screen was empty, wiped clean during a single scan of the beam. The creature had fallen below our horizon, and was hidden from us now by the curve of the planet. Far out in the burning dayside of Mercury, in the inferno where only a dozen men have ever ventured and fewer still come back alive, it smashed silently and invisibly against the seas of molten metal, the hills of slowly moving lava. The mere impact could have meant nothing to such an entity* what it could not endure was its first contact with the inconceivable cold of solid matter.

Yes, cold. It had descended upon the hottest spot in the solar system, where the temperature never falls below several hundred degrees Fahrenheit and sometimes approaches thousand. And that was far, far colder to it than the antarctic winter would be to a naked man.

We did not see it die, out there in the freezing fire; it was beyond the reach of our instruments now, and none of them recorded its end. Yet every one of us knew when that moment came, and that is why we are not interested when those who have seen only the films and tapes tell us that we were watching some purely natural phenomenon.

How can one explain what we felt, in that last moment when half our little world was enmeshed in the dissolving tendrils of that huge but immaterial brain? I can only say that it was a soundless cry of anguish, a death pang that seeped into our minds without passing through the gateways of the senses. Not one of us doubted then, or has ever doubted since, that he had witnessed the passing of a giant.

We may have been both the first and the last of all men to see so mighty a fall. Whatever they may be, in their unimaginable world within the sun, our paths and theirs may never cross again. It is hard to see how we can ever make contact with them, even if their intelligence matches ours.

And does it? It may be well for us if we never know the answer. Perhaps they have been living there inside the sun since the universe was born and have climbed to peaks of wisdom that we shall never scale. The future may be theirs, not ours; already they may be talking across the light-years to their cousins in other stars.

One day they may discover us, by whatever strange senses they possess, as we circle around their mighty, ancient home, proud of our knowledge and thinking ourselves lords of creation. They may not like what they find, for to them we should be no more than maggots, crawling upon the skins of worlds too cold to cleanse themselves from the corruption of organic life.

And then, if they have the power, they will do what they consider necessary. The sun will put forth its strength and lick the faces of its children; and thereafter the planets will go their way once more as they were in the beginning-clean and bright... and sterile.

The Pacifist

I got to the "White Hart" late that evening, and when I arrived everyone was crowded into the comer under the dartboard. All exceptDrew, that is: he had not deserted his post, but was sitting behind the bar reading the collected T. S. Eliot. He broke off from "The Confidential Clerk" long enough to hand me a beer and to tell me what was going on.

"Eric's brought in some kind of games machine-it's beaten everybody so far. Sam's trying his luck with it now."

At that moment a roar of laughter announced that Sam had been no luckier than the rest, and I pushed my way through the crowd to see what was happening.

On the table lay a flat metal box the size of a checkerboard, and divided into squares in a similar way. At the corner of each squarewas a two-way switch and a little neon lamp: the whole affair was plugged into the light socket (thus plunging the dartboard into darkness) and Eric Rodgers was looking round for a new victim.

"What does the thing do?" I asked.

"It's a modification of naughts ; and crosses-what the Americans call Tic-Tac-Toe.Shannon showed it to me when I was over at Bell Labs. What you have to do is to complete a path from one side of the board to the other-call itNorth to South-by turning these switches. Imagine the thing forms a grid of streets, if you like, and these neons are the traffic lights. You and the machine take turns making moves. The machine tries to block your path by building one of its own in the East-West direction-the little neons light up to tell youwhich way it wants to make a move. Neither track need be a straight line: you can zig-zag as much as you like.

All that matters is that the path must be continuous, and the one togot across the board first wins."

All that matters is that the path must be continuous, and the one togot across the board first wins."

"Well, it's never been beaten yet."

"Can't you force a draw, by blocking the machine's path, so that at least you don't lose?"

"That's what we're trying: like to have a go?"

Two minutes later I joined the other unsuccessful contestants. The machine had dodged all my barriers and established its own track from East to West. I wasn't convinced that it was unbeatable, but the game was clearly a good deal more complicated than it looked.

Eric glanced round his audience when I had retired. No-one else seemed in a hurry to move forward.

"Ha!" he said."The very man. What about you, Purvis? You've not had a shot yet."

Harry Purvis was standing at the back of the crowd, with a faraway look in his eye. He jolted back to earth as Eric addressed him, but didn't answer the question directly.

"Fascinating things, these electronic computers," he mused. "I suppose I shouldn't tell you this, but your gadget reminds me of what happened to Project Clausewitz . A curiousstory, and one very expensive to the American taxpayer."

"Look," said John Wyndham anxiously. "Before you start,be a good sport and let us get our glasses filled. Drew!"

This important matter having been attended to, we gathered round Harry. Only Charlie Willis still remained with the machine, hopefully trying his luck.

"As you all know," began Harry, "Science with a capital S is a big thing in the military world these days. The weapons side-rockets, atom bombs and so on-is only part of it, though that's all the public knows about. Much more fascinating, in my opinion, is the operational research angle. You might say that's concerned with brains rather than brute force. I once heard it defined as how to win wars without actually fighting, and that's not a bad description.

"Now you all know about the big electronic computers thatCropped up like mushrooms in the 1950's. Most of them were built to deal with mathematical problems, but when you think about itYou'll realise that War itself is a mathematical problem. It's such a complicated one that human brains can't handle it-there are far too many variables. Even the greatest strategist cannot see the picture as a whole: the Hiders and Napoleons always make a mistake in the end.

But a machine-that would be a different matter. A number of bright people realized this after the end of the war. The techniques that had been worked out in the building of ENIAC and the other big computers could revolutionize strategy.

"Hence Project Clausewitz .Don't ask me how I got to know about it, or press me for too many details. All that matters is that a good many megabucks worth of electronic equipment, and some of the best scientific brains in the United States, went into a certain cavern in the Kentucky hills. They're still there, but things haven't turned out exactly as they expected.

"Now I don't know what experience you have of high-ranking military officers, but there's one type you've all come across in fiction. That's the pompous, conservative, stick-in-the-mud careerist who's got to the top by sheer pressure from beneath, who does everything by rules and regulations and regards civilians as, at the best, unfriendly neutrals. I'll let you into a secret: he actually exists. He's not very common nowadays, but he's still around and sometimes it's not possible to find a safe job for him. When that happens, he's worth his weight in plutonium to the Other Side.

"Now I don't know what experience you have of high-ranking military officers, but there's one type you've all come across in fiction. That's the pompous, conservative, stick-in-the-mud careerist who's got to the top by sheer pressure from beneath, who does everything by rules and regulations and regards civilians as, at the best, unfriendly neutrals. I'll let you into a secret: he actually exists. He's not very common nowadays, but he's still around and sometimes it's not possible to find a safe job for him. When that happens, he's worth his weight in plutonium to the Other Side.

"Of course, he was only concerned with the administrative, not the scientific, aspects of the work. All might yet have been well had the General been content to let the scientists get on with their work while he concentrated on saluting smartness, the coefficient of reflection of barrack floors, and similar matters of military importance. Unfortunately, he didn't.

"The General had led a sheltered existence. He had, if I may borrow from Wilde (everybody else does) been a man of peace, except in his domestic life. He had never met scientists before, and the shock was considerable. So perhaps it is not fair to blame him for everything that happened.

"It was a considerable time before he realised the aims and objects of Project Clausewitz , and when he did he was quite disturbed. This may have made him feel even less friendly towards his scientific staff, for despite anything I may have said the General was not entirely a fool. He was intelligent enough to understand that, if the Project succeeded, there might be more ex-generals around than even the combined boards of management of American industry could comfortably absorb.

"But let's leave the General for a minute and have a look at the scientists. There were about fifty of them, as well as a couple of hundred technicians. They'd all been carefully screened by the F.B.I., so probably not more than half a dozen were active members of the Communist Party. Though there was a lot of talk of sabotage later, for once in a while the comrades were completely innocent. Besides, what happened certainly wasn't sabotage in any generally accepted meaning of the word . . . .

"The man who had really designed the computer was a quiet little mathematical genius who had been swept out of college into the Kentucky hills and the world of Security and Priorities before he'd really realized what had happened. He wasn't called Dr. Milquetoast, but he should have been and that's what it christen him.

"To complete our cast of characters, I'd better say something about Karl. At this stage in the business, Karl was only half-built. Like all big computers, most of him consisted of vast banks of memory units which could receive and store information until it was needed. The creative part of Karl's brain-the analyzers, and integrators-took this information and operated on it, to produce answers to the questions he was asked. Given all the relevant facts, Karl would produce the right answers. The problem, of course, was to see that Karl did have all the facts-he couldn't be expected to get the right results from inaccurate or insufficient information.

"It was Dr. Milquetoast's responsibility to design Karl's brain. Yes, I know that's a crudely anthropomorphic way of looking at it, but no-one can deny that these big computers have personalities.

It's hard to put it more accurately without getting technical, so I'll simply say that little Milquetoast had to reate the extremely

"So here are our three protagonists-General Smith, pining for the days of Custer; Dr. Milquetoast, lost in the fascinating scientific intricacies of his job; and Karl, fifty tons of electronic gear, not yet animated by the currents that would soon be coursing through him.

"Soon-but not soon enough for General Smith. Let's not be too hard on the General: someone had probably put the pressure on him, when it became obvious that the Project was falling behind schedule. He called Dr. Milquetoast into his office.

"The interview lasted more than thirty minutes, and the doctor said less than thirty words. Most of the time the General was making pointed remarks about production times, deadlines and bottlenecks. He seemed to be under the impression that building Karl differed in no important particular from the assembly of the current model Ford: it was just a question of putting the bits together. Dr. Milquetoast was not the sort of man to explain the error, even if the General had given him the opportunity. He left, smarting under a considerable sense of injustice.

"A week later, it was obvious that the creation of Karl was falling still further behind schedule. Milquetoast was doing his best, and there was no-one who could do better. Problems of a complexity totally beyond the General's comprehension had to be met and mastered. They were4nastered, but it took time, and time was in short supply.

"At his first interview, the General had tried to be as nice as he could, and had succeeded in being merely rude. This time, he tried to be rude, with results that I leave to your imagination. He practically insinuated that Milquetoast and his colleagues, by falling behind their deadlines, were guilty of un-American inactivity.

"From this moment onwards, two things started to happen. Relations between the Army and the scientists grew steadily worse; and Dr. Milquetoast, for the first time, began to give serious thought to the wider implications of his work. HeLd always been too busy, too engaged upon the immediate problems of his task, to consider his social responsibilities. He was still too busy now, but that didn't stop him pausing for reflection. 'Here am I,' he told himself, 'one of the best pure mathematicians in the world-and whatam I doing? What's happened to my thesis on Diophantine equations? When am I going to have another smack at the prime number theorem? In short, when am I going to do some real work again?

"He could have resigned, but that didn't occur to him. In any case, far down beneath that mild and diffident exterior was a stubborn streak. Dr. Milquetoast continued to work, even more energetically than before. The construction of Karl proceeded slowly but steadily: the final connexions in his myriad-celled brain were soldered: the thousands of circuits were checked and tested by the mechanics.

"And one circuit, indistinguishably interwoven among its multitude of companions and leading to a set of memory cells apparently identical with all the others, was tested by Dr. Milquetoast alone, for no-one else knew that it existed.

"The great day came. To Kentucky, by devious routes, came very important personages. A whole constellation of multi-starred generals arrived from the Pentagon. Even the Navy had been invited.

"Proudly, General Smith led the visitors from cavern to cavern, from memory banks to selector networks to matrix analyzers to input tables-and finally to the rows of electric typewriters on which Karl would print the results of his deliberations. The General knew his way around quite well: at least, he got most of the names right. He even managed to give the impression, to those who knew no better, that he was largely responsible for Karl.

"At the word 'sums' the mathematicians winced, but the General was unaware of his faux pas. The assembled brass thought for a while: then someone said daringly, 'What's 9 multiplied byitself twenty times?

"One of the technicians, with an audible sniff, punched a few keys. There was a rattle of gunfire from an electric typewriter, and before anyone could blink twice the answer had appeared-all twenty digits of it."

(I've looked it up since: for anyone who wants to know it's:12157665459056928801

But let's get back to Harry and his tale.)

"For the next fifteen minutes Karl was bombarded with similar trivialities. The visitors were impressed, though there was no reason to suppose that the'd have spotted it if all the answers had been 'Y completely wrong.

"The General gave a modest cough. Simple arithmetic was as far as he could go, and Karl had barely begun to warm up. 'I'll now hand you over,' he said, 'to Captain Winkler.'

"Captain Winkler was an intense young Harvard graduate whom the General distrusted, rightly suspecting him to be more a scientist than a military man. But he was the only officer who really understood what Karl was supposed to do, or could explain exactly how he set about doing it. He looked, the General thought grumpily, like a damned schoolmaster as he started to lecture the visitors.

"The tactical problem that had been set up was a complicated one, but the answer was already known to everybody except Karl. It was a battle that had been fought and finished almost a century before, and when Captain Winkler concluded his introduction, a general from Boston whispered to his side, 'I'll bet some damn Southerner has fixed it so that Lee wins this time.' Everyone had to admit, however, that the problem was an excellent way of testing Karl's capabilities.

"The punched tapes disappeared into the capacious memory units: patterns of lights flickered and flashed across the registers; mysterious things happened in all directions.

"'This problem,' said Captain Winkler primly, 'will take about five minutes to evaluate.)

"As if in deliberate contradiction, one of the typewriters promptly started to chatter. A strip of paper shot out of the feed, and Captain Winkler, looking rather puzzled at Karl's unexpected alacrity, read the message. His lower jaw immediately dropped six inches, and he stood staring at the paper as if unable to believe his eyes.

"'What is it, man?barked the General.

"Captain Winkler swallowed hard, but appeared to have lost the power of speech. With a snort of impatience, the General snatched the paper from him. Then it was his turn to stand paralyzed, but unlike his subordinate he also turned a most beautiful red. For a moment he looked like some tropical fish strangling out of water: then, not without a slight scuffle, the enigmatic message impatience, the General snatched the paper from him. Then it was his turn to stand paralyzed, but unlike his subordinate he also turned a most beautiful red. For a moment he looked like some tropical fish strangling out of water: then, not without a slight scuffle, the enigmatic message "His reaction was totally different. He promptly doubled up with laughter.

"The minor officers were left in a state of infuriating suspense for quite ten minutes. But finally the news filtered down through Colonels to Captains to Lieutenants, until at last there wasn't a G.I. in the establishment who did not know the wonderful news.

"Karl had told General Smith that he was a pompous baboon. That was all.

"Even though everybody agreed with Karl, the matter could hardly be allowed to rest there. Something, obviously, had gone wrong. Something-or someone-had diverted Karl's attention from the Battle of Gettysburg.

"'Where,' roared General Smith, finally recovering his voice, 'is Dr. Milquetoast?'

"He was no longer present. He had slipped quietly out of the room, having witnessed his great moment. Retribution would come later, of course, but it was worth it.

"The frantic technicians cleared the circuits and started running tests. They gave Karl an elaborate series of multiplications and divisions to perform-the computer's equivalent of 'The quick brown fox jumps over the lazy dog.' Everything seemed to be functioning perfectly. So, they put in a very simple tactical problem, which a Lieutenant J. G. could solve in his sleep.

"Said Karl: 'Go jump in a lake, General.'

"It was then that General Smith realised that he was confronted with something outside the scope of Standard Operating Procedure. He was faced with mechanical mutiny, no less.

"It took several hours of tests to discover exactly what had happened. Somewhere tucked away in Karl's capacious memory units was a superb collection of insults, lovingly assembled by Dr. Milquetoast. He had punched on tape, or recorded in patterns of electrical impulses, I everything he would like to have said to the General himself. But that was not all he had done: that would have been too easy, not worthy of his genius. He had also installed what could only be called a censor circuit-he had given Karl the power of discrimination. Before solving it, Karl examined every problem fed to him. If it was concerned with pure mathematics, he co-operated and dealt with it properly. But if it was a military problem -out came one of the insults. After twenty times, he had not repeated himself once, and the Waco's had already had to be sent out of the room.

"It must be confessed that after a while the technicians were almost as interested in discovering what indignity Karl would next heap upon General Smith as they were in finding the fault in the circuits. He had begun with mere insults and surprising geneological surmises, but had swiftly passed on to detailed instructions the mildest of which would have been highly prejudicial to the General's dignity, while the more imaginative would have seriously imperiled his physical integrity.The fact that all these messages, as they emerged from the typewriters, were immediately classified TOP SECRET was small consolation to the recipient. He knew with a glum certainty that this would be the worst-kept secret of the cold war, and that it was time he looked round for a civilian occupation.

"And there, gentlemen," concluded Purvis, "the situation remains. The engineers are still trying to unravel the circuits that Dr. Milquetoast installed, and no doubt it's only a matter of time before they succeed. But meanwhile Karl remains an unyielding pacifist. He's perfectly happy playing with the theory of numbers, computing tables of powers, and handling arithmetical problems generally. Do you remember the famous toast 'Here's to pure mathematics may it never be of any use to anybody'? Karl would have seconded that . . .

"As for Dr. Milquetoast, no one could do much about him because he promptly had a nervous breakdown. It was suspiciously well timed, but he could certainly claim to have earned it. When last heard of he was teaching matrix algebra at a theological college inDenver . He swears he's forgotten everything that had ever happened while he was working on Karl. Maybe he was even telling the truth . . "

There was a sudden shout from the back of the room.

"I've won!" cried Charles Willis. "Come and see!"

We all crowded under the dartboard. It seemed true enough. Charlie had established a zig-zag but continuous track from one side of the checker-board to the other, despite the obstacles the machine had tried to put in his way.

"Show us how you did it," said Eric Rodgers.

Charlie looked embarrassed.

"I've forgotten," he said. "I didn't make a note of all the moves."

A sarcastic voice broke in from the background.

"But I did," said John Christopher. "You were cheating-you made two moves at once."

After that, I am sorry to say, there was some disorder, and Drew had to threaten violence before peace was restored. I don't know who really won the squabble, and I don't think it matters. For I'm inclined to agree with what Purvis remarked as he picked up the robot checker-board and examined its wiring.

"You see," he said, "this little gadget is only a simple-minded cousin of Karl's-andlook what it's done already. All these machines are beginning to make us look fools. Before long they'll start to disobey us without any Milquetoast interfering with their circuits. And then they'll start ordering us about-they're logical, after all, and won't stand any nonsense."

He sighed. "When that happens, there won't be a thing we can do about it. We'll just have to say to the dinosaurs: 'Move over a bit-herecomes homo sap!' And the transistor shall inherit the earth."

There was no time for further pessimistic philosophy, for the door opened and Police Constable Wilkins stuck his head in. "Where's the owner of CGC 571?" he asked testily. "Oh-it's you, Mr. Purvis. Your rear light's out." Harry looked at me sadly, then shrugged his shoulders in resignation. "You see," he said, "it's started already." And he went out into the night.

The Possessed

And now the sun ahead was so close that the hurricane of radiation was forcing the Swarm back into the dark night of space. Soon it would be able to come no closer; the gales of light on which it rode from star to star could not be faced so near their source. Unless it encountered a planet very soon, and could fall down into the peace and safety of its shadow, this sun must be abandoned as had so many before.

Six cold outer worlds had already been searched and discarded. Either they were frozen beyond all hope of organic life, or else they harboured entities of types that were useless to the Swarm. If it was to survive, it must find hosts not too unlike those it had left on its doomed and distant home. Millions of years ago the Swarm had begun its journey, swept starward by the fires of its own exploding sun. Yet even now the memory of its lost birthplace was still sharp and clear, an ache that would never die. There was a planet ahead, swinging its cone of shadow through the flame-swept night. The senses that the Swarm had developed upon its long journey reached out toward the approaching world, reached out and found it good.

The merciless buffeting of radiation ceased as the black disc of the planet eclipsed the sun. Falling freely under gravity, the Swarm dropped swiftly until it hit the outer fringe of the atmosphere. The first time it had made planetfall it had almost met its doom, but now it contracted its tenuous substance with the unthinking skill of long practice, until it formed a tiny, close-knit sphere. Slowly its velocity slackened, until at last it was floating motionless between earth and sky.

For many years it rode the winds of the stratosphere from Pole to Pole, or let the soundless fusillades of dawn blast it westward from the rising sun. Everywhere it found life, but nowhere intelligence. There were things that crawled and flew and leaped, but there were no things that talked or built. Ten million years hence there might be creatures here with minds that the Swarm could possess and guide for its own purposes; there was no sign of them now. It could not guess which of the countless life-forms on this planet would be the heir to the future, and without such a host it was helpless--a mere pattern of electric charges, a matrix of order and self-awareness in a universe of chaos. By its own resources the Swarm had no control over matter, yet once it had lodged in the mind of a sentient race there was nothing that lay beyond its powers. It was not the first time, and it would not be the last, that the planet had been surveyed by a visitant from space--though never by one in such peculiar and urgent need. The Swarm was faced with a tormenting dilemma. It could begin its weary travels once more, hoping that ultimately it might find the conditions it sought, or it could wait here on this world, biding its time until a race had arisen which would fit its purpose. It moved like mist through the shadows, letting the vagrant winds take it where they willed. The clumsy, ill-formed reptiles of this young world never saw its passing, but it observed them, recording, analysing, trying to extrapolate into the future. There was so little to choose between all these creatures; not one showed even the first faint glimmerings of conscious mind. Yet if it left this world in search of another, it might roam the Universe in vain until the end of time.

At last it made its decision. By its very nature, it could choose both alternatives. The greater part of the Swarm would continue its travels among the stars, but a portion of it would remain on this world, like a seed planted in the hope of future harvest. It began to spin upon its axis, its tenuous body flattening into a disc. Now it was wavering at the frontiers of visibility--it was a pale ghost, a faint will-o'-the-wisp that suddenly fissured into two unequal fragments. The spinning slowly died away: the Swarm had become two, each an entity with all the memories of the original, and all its desires and needs.

There was a last exchange of thoughts between parent and child who were also identical twins. If all went well with them both, they would meet again in the far future here at this valley in the mountains. The one who was staying would return to this point at regular intervals down the ages; the one who continued the search would send back an emissary if ever a better world was found. And then they would be united again, no longer homeless exiles vainly wandering among the indifferent stars.

The light of dawn was spilling over the raw, new mountains when the parent swarm rose up to meet the sun. At the edge of the atmosphere the gales of radiation caught it and swept it unresisting out beyond the planets, to start again upon the endless search.

The one that was left began its almost equally hopeless task. It needed an animal that was not so rare that disease or accident could make it extinct, nor so tiny that it could never acquire any power over the physical world. And it must breed rapidly, so that its evolution could be directed and controlled as swiftly as possible. The search was long and the choice difficult, but at last the Swarm selected its host. Like rain sinking into thirsty soil, it entered the bodies of certain small lizards and began to direct their destiny.

It was an immense task, even for a being which could never know death.

Generation after generation of the lizards was swept into the past before there came the slightest improvement in the race. And always, at the appointed time, the Swarm returned to its rendezvous among the mountains. Always it returned in vain: there was no messenger from the stars, bringing news of better fortune elsewhere.

The centuries lengthened into millennia, the millennia into eons. By the standards of geological time, the lizards were now changing rapidly. Presently they were lizards no more, but warm-blooded, fur-covered creatures that brought forth their young alive. They were still small and feeble, and their minds were rudimentary, but they contained the seeds of future greatness. Yet not only the living creatures were altering as the ages slowly passed.

Continents were being rent asunder, mountains being worn down by the weight of the unwearying rain. Through all these changes, the Swarm kept to its purpose; and always, at the appointed times, it went to the meeting place that had been chosen so long ago, waited patiently for a while, and came away. Perhaps the parent swarm was still searching or perhaps--it was a hard and terrible thought to grasp--some unknown fate had overtaken it and it had gone the way of the race it had once ruled. There was nothing to do but to wait and see if the stubborn life-stuff of this planet could be forced along the path to intelligence.

And so the eons passed....

Somewhere in the labyrinth of evolution the Swarm made its fatal mistake and took the wrong turning. A hundred million years had gone since it came to Earth, and it was very weary. It could not die, but it could degenerate. The memories of its ancient home and of its destiny were fading: its intelligence was waning even while its hosts climbed the long slope that would lead to self-awareness.

By a cosmic irony, in giving the impetus which would one day bring intelligence to this world, the Swarm had exhausted itself. It had reached the last stage of parasitism; no longer could it exist apart from its hosts. Never again could it ride free above the world, driven by wind and sun. To make the pilgrimage to the ancient rendezvous, it must travel slowly and painfully in a thousand little bodies. Yet it continued the immemorial custom, driven on by the desire for reunion which burned all the more fiercely now that it knew the bitterness of failure. Only if the parent swarm returned and reabsorbed it could it ever know new life and vigour.

The glaciers came and went; by a miracle the little beasts that now housed the waning alien intelligence escaped the clutching fingers of the ice. The oceans overwhelmed the land, and still the race survived. It even multiplied, but it could do no more. This world would never be its heritage, for far away in the heart of another continent a certain monkey had come down from the trees and was looking at the stars with the first glimmerings of curiosity.

The mind of the Swarm was dispersing, scattering among a million tiny bodies, no longer able to unite and assert its will. It had lost all cohesion; its memories were fading. In a million years, at most, they would all be gone.

Only one thing remained--the blind urge which still, at intervals which by some strange aberration were becoming ever shorter, drove it to seek its consummation in a valley that long ago had ceased to exist.

Quietly riding the lane of moonlight, the pleasure steamer passed the island with its winking beacon and entered the fjord. It was a calm and lovely night, with Venus sinking in the west out beyond the Faroes, and the lights of the harbour reflected with scarcely a tremor in the still waters far ahead.

Nils and Christina were utterly content. Standing side by side against the boat rail, their fingers locked together, they watched the wooded slopes drift silently by. The tall trees were motionless in the moonlight, their leaves unruffled by even the merest breath of wind, their slender trunks rising whitely from pools of shadow. The whole world was asleep; only the moving ship dared to break the spell that had bewitched the night.

Then suddenly, Christina gave a little gasp and Nils felt her fingers tighten convulsively on his. He followed her gaze: she was staring out across the water, looking toward the silent sentinels of the forest. "What is it, darling?" he asked anxiously.

"Look!" she replied, in a whisper Nils could scarcely hear. "There-- under the pines!"

Nils stared, and as he did so the beauty of the night ebbed slowly away and ancestral terrors came crawling back from exile. For beneath the trees the land was alive: a dappled brown tide was moving down the slopes of the hill and merging into the dark waters. Here was an open patch on which the moonlight fell unbroken by shadow. It was changing even as he watched: the surface of the land seemed to be rippling downward like a slow waterfall seeking union with the sea.

And then Nils laughed and the world was sane once more. Christina looked at him, puzzled but reassured.

"Don't you remember?" he chuckled. "We read all about it in the paper this morning. They do this every few years, and always at night. It's been going on for days." He was teasing her, sweeping away the tension of the last few minutes. Christina looked back at him, and a slow smile lit up her face.

"Of course!" she said. "How stupid of me!" Then she turned once more toward the land and her expression became sad, for she was very tenderhearted.

"Poor little things!" she sighed. "I wonder why they do it?" Nils shrugged his shoulders indifferently.

"No one knows," he answered. "It's just one of those mysteries. I shouldn't think about it if it worries you. Look--we'll soon be in harbour!"

They turned toward the beckoning lights where their future lay, and Christina glanced back only once toward the tragic, mindless tide that was still flowing beneath the moon.

Obeying an urge whose meaning they had never known, the doomed legions of the lemmings were finding oblivion beneath the waves.

The Reluctant Orchid

Science fiction, it has often been pointed out, is sadly lacking in humour. But something is worthwhile only if one can make fun of it, and this I set out to do in Tales from the "White Hart." There is nothing fictitious about the White Hart, or most of its clientele. Imitation is the sincerest form of flattery, and I would like to pay here a tribute to the memory of Lord Dunsany, who was very kind to me in the early nineteen-fifties. There is undoubtedly a family resemblance between Harry Purvis and his Mr. Jorkens. Though few people in the "White Hart" will concede that any of Harry Purvis' stories are actually true, everyone agrees that some are much more probable than others. And on any scale of probability, the affair of the Reluctant Orchid must rate very low indeed. I don't remember what ingenious gambit Harry used to launch this narrative: maybe some orchid fancier brought his latest monstrosity into the bar, and that set him off. No matter. I do remember the story, and after all that's what counts.

The adventure did not, this time, concern any of Harry's numerous relatives, and he avoided explaining just how he managed to know so many of the sordid details. The hero--if you can call him that--of this hothouse epic was an inoffensive little clerk named Hercules Keating. And if you think that is the most unlikely part of the story, just stick round a while.

Hercules is not the sort of name you can carry off lightly at the best of times, and when you are four foot nine and look a if you'd have to take a physical-culture course before you can even become a ninety-seven-pound weakling, it is a positive embarrassment. Perhaps it helped to explain why Hercule had very little social life, and all his real friends grew in pots in a humid conservatory at the bottom of his garden. His needs were simple and he spent very little money on himself; consequently his collection of orchids and cacti was really rather remarkable. Indeed, he had a wide reputation among the fraternity of cactophiles, and often received from remote corners of the globe parcels smelling of mould and tropical jungles.

Hercules had only one living relative, and it would have been hard to find a greater contrast than Aunt Henrietta She was a massive six-footer, usually wore a rather loud line in Harris tweeds, drove a Jaguar with reckless skill, and chain-smoked cigars. Her parents had set their hearts on a boy, and had never been able to decide whether or not their wish had been granted. Henrietta earned a living, and quite a good one, breeding dogs of various shapes and sizes. She was seldom without a couple of her latest models, and they were not the type of portable canine which ladies like to carry in their handbags. The Keating Kennels specialised in Great Danes, Alsatians, and Saint Bernards.,..

Henrietta, rightly despising men as the weaker sex, had never married. However, for some reason she took an avuncular (yes, that is definitely the right word) interest in Hercules, and called to see him almost every weekend. It was a curious kind of relationship: probably Henrietta found that Hercules bolstered up her feelings of superiority. If he was a good example of the male sex, then they were certainly a pretty sorry lot. Yet, if this was Henrietta's motivation, she was unconscious of it and seemed genuinely fond of her nephew. She was patronising, but never unkind.

As might be expected, her attentions did not exactly help Hercules' own welldeveloped inferiority complex. At first he had tolerated his aunt; then he came to dread her regular visits, her booming voice, and her bone-crushing handshake; and at last he grew to hate her. Eventually, indeed, his hate was the dominant emotion in his life, exceeding even his love for his orchids. But he was careful not to show it, realising that if Aunt Henrietta discovered how he felt about her, she would probably break him in two and throw the pieces to her wolf pack.

There was no way, then, in which Hercules could express his pent-up feelings. He had to be polite to Aunt Henrietta even when he felt like murder. And he often did feel like murder, though he knew that there was nothing he would ever do about it. Until one day...

According to the dealer, the orchid came from "somewhere in the Amazon region"--a rather vague postal address. When Hercules first saw it, it was not a very prepossessing sight, even to anyone who loved orchids as much as he did. A shapeless root, about the size of a man's fist--that was all. It was redolent of decay, and there was the faintest hint of a rank, carrion smell. Hercules was not even sure that it was viable, and told the dealer as much. Perhaps that enabled him to purchase it for a trifling sum, and he carried it home without much enthusiasm.

It showed no signs of life for the first month, but that did not worry Hercules. Then, one day, a tiny green shoot appeared and started to creep up to the light. After that, progress was rapid. Soon there was a thick, fleshy stem as big as a man's forearm, and coloured a positively virulent green. Near the top of the stem a series of curious bulges circled the plant: otherwise it was completely featureless. Hercules was now quite excited: he was sure that some entirely new species had swum into his ken. The rate of growth was now really fantastic: soon the plant was taller than Hercules, not that that was saying a great deal. Moreover, the bulges seemed to be developing, and it looked as if at any moment the orchid would burst into bloom. Hercules waited anxiously, knowing how short-lived some flowers can be, and spent as much time as he possibly could in the hothouse. Despite all his watchfulness, the transformation occurred one night while he was asleep.

In the morning, the orchid was fringed by a series of eight dangling tendrils, almost reaching to the ground. They must have developed inside the plant and emerged with--for the vegetable world-- explosive speed. Hercules stared at the phenomenon in amazement, and went very thoughtfully to work.

That evening, as he watered the plant and checked its soil, he noticed a still more peculiar fact. The tendrils were thickening, and they were not completely motionless. They had a slight but unmistakable tendency to vibrate, as if possessing a life of their own. Even Hercules, for all his interest and enthusiasm, found this more than a little disturbing.

A few days later, there was no doubt about it at all. When he approached the orchid, the tendrils swayed toward him in an unpleasantly suggestive fashion. The impression of hunger was so strong that Hercules began to feel very uncomfortable indeed, and something started to nag at the back of his mind. It was quite a while before he could recall what it was: then he said to himself, "Of course! How stupid of me!" and went along to the local library. Here he spent a most interesting half hour rereading a little piece by one H. G. Wells entitled, "The Flowering of the Strange Orchid." "My goodness!" thought Hercules, when he had finished the tale. As yet there had been no stupefying odour which might overpower the plant's intended victim, but otherwise the characteristics were all too similar. Hercules went home in a very unsettled mood indeed.

He opened the conservatory door and stood looking along the avenue of greenery toward his prize specimen. He judged the length of the tendrils--already he found himself calling them tentacles--with great care and walked to within what appeared a safe distance. The plant certainly had an impression of alertness and menace far more appropriate to the animal than the vegetable kingdom. Hercules remembered the unfortunate history of Doctor Frankenstein, and was not amused. But, really, this was ridiculous! Such things didn't happen in real life. Well, there was one way to put matters to the test....

Hercules went into the house and came back a few minutes later with a broomstick, to the end of which he had attached a piece of raw meat. Feeling a considerable fool, he advanced toward the orchid as a lion tamer might approach one of his charges at mealtime.

For a moment, nothing happened. Then two of the tendrils developed an agitated twitch. They began to sway back and forth, as if the plant was making up its mind. Abruptly, they whipped out with such speed that they practically vanished from view. They wrapped themselves round the meat, and Hercules felt a powerful tug at the end of his broomstick. Then the meat was gone: the orchid was clutching it, if one may mix metaphors slightly, to its bosom.

"Jumping Jehosophat!" yelled Hercules. It was very seldom indeed that he used such strong language.

The orchid showed no further signs of life for twenty-four hours. It was waiting for the meat to become high, and it was also developing its digestive system. By the next day, a network of what looked like short roots had covered the still-visible chunk of meat. By nightfall, the meat was gone.

The plant had tasted blood.

Hercules' emotions as he watched over his prize were curiously mixed. There were times when it almost gave him nightmares, and he foresaw a whole range of horrid possibilities. The orchid was now extremely strong, and if he got within its clutches he would be done for. But, of course, there was not the slightest danger of that. He had arranged a system of pipes so that it could be watered from a safe distance, and its less orthodox food he simply tossed within range of its tentacles. It was now eating a pound of raw meat a day, and he had an uncomfortable feeling that it could cope with much larger quantities if given the opportunity.

Hercules' natural qualms were, on the whole, outweighed by his feeling of triumph that such a botanical marvel had fallen into his hands. Whenever he chose, he could become the most famous orchid-grower in the world. It was typical of his somewhat restricted viewpoint that it never occurred to him that other people besides orchid fanciers might be interested in his pet.

The creature was now about six feet tall, and apparently still growing--though much more slowly than it had been. All the other plants had been moved from its end of the conservatory, not so much because Hercules feared that it might be cannibalistic as to enable him to tend them without danger. He had stretched a rope across the central aisle so that there was no risk of his accidentally walking within range of those eight dangling arms.

It was obvious that the orchid had a highly developed nervous system, and something very nearly approaching intelligence. It knew when it was going to be fed, and exhibited unmistakable signs of pleasure. Most fantastic of all--though Hercules was still not sure about this--it seemed capable of producing sounds. There were times, just before a meal, when he fancied he could hear an incredibly high-pitched whistle, skirting the edge of audibility. A newborn bat might have had such a voice: he wondered what purpose it served. Did the orchid somehow lure its prey into its clutches by sound? If so, he did not think the technique would work on him.

While Hercules was making these interesting discoveries, he continued to be fussed over by Aunt Henrietta and assaulted by her hounds, which were never as housetrained as she claimed them to be. She would usually roar up the street on a Sunday afternoon with one dog in the seat beside her and another occupying most of the baggage compartment. Then she would bound up the steps two at a time, nearly deafen Hercules with her greeting, half paralyse him with her handshake, and blow cigar smoke in his face. There had been a time when he was terrified that she would kiss him, but he had long since realised that such effeminate behaviour was foreign to her nature. Aunt Henrietta looked upon Hercules' orchids with some scorn. Spending one's spare time in a hothouse was, she considered, a very effete recreation. When she wanted to let off steam, she went big-game hunting in Kenya. This did nothing to endear her to Hercules, who hated blood sports. But despite his mounting dislike for his overpowering aunt, every Sunday afternoon he dutifully prepared tea for her and they had a tête-á-tête together which, on the surface at least, seemed perfectly friendly. Henrietta never guessed that as he poured the tea Hercules often wished it was poisoned: she was, far down beneath her extensive fortifications, a fundamentally goodhearted person and the knowledge would have upset her deeply.

Hercules did not mention his vegetable octopus to Aunt Henrietta. He had occasionally shown her his most interesting specimens, but this was something he was keeping to himself. Perhaps, even before he had fully formulated his diabolical plan, his subconscious was already preparing the ground....

It was late one Sunday evening, when the roar of the Jaguar had died away into the night and Hercules was restoring his shattered nerves in the conservatory, that the idea first came fully fledged into his mind. He was staring at the orchid, noting how the tendrils were now as thick around as a man's thumb, when a most pleasing fantasy suddenly flashed before his eyes. He pictured Aunt Henrietta struggling helplessly in the grip of the monster, unable to escape from its carnivorous clutches. Why, it would be the perfect crime. The distraught nephew would arrive on the scene too late to be of assistance, and when the police answered his frantic call they would see at a glance that the whole affair was a deplorable accident. True, there would be an inquest, but the coroner's censure would be toned down in view of Hercules' obvious grief.... The more he thought of the idea, the more he liked it. He could see no flaws, as long as the orchid co-operated. That clearly, would be the greatest problem. He would have to plaa a course of training for the creature. It already looked sui ciently diabolical; he must give it a disposition to suit its a pearance.

Considering that he had no prior experience in such matters, and that there were no authorities he could consult, Hercules proceeded along very sound and businesslike lines. He would use a fishing rod to dangle pieces of meat just outside the orchid's range, until the creature lashed its tentacles in a frenzy. At such times its high-pitched squeak was clearly audible, and Hercules wondered how it managed to produce the sound. He also wondered what its organs of perception were, but this was yet another mystery that could not be solve without close examination. Perhaps Aunt Henrietta, if all went well, would have a brief opportunity of discovering these interesting facts--though she would probably be too busy report them for the benefit of posterity.

There was no doubt that the beast was quite powerful enough to deal with its intended victim. It had once wrenched a broomstick out of Hercules' grip, and although that in itself proved very little, the sickening "crack" of the wood a moment later brought a smile of satisfaction to its trainer's thin lips. He began to be much more pleasant and attentive to his aunt. In every respect, indeed, he was the model nephew. When Hercules considered that his picador tactics had brought the orchid into the right frame of mind, he wondered if he should test it with live bait. This was a problem that worried him for some weeks, during which time he would look speculatively at every dog or cat he passed in the street, but he finally abandoned the idea, for a rather peculiar reason. He was simply too kindhearted to put it into practice. Aunt Henrietta would have to be the first victim.

He starved the orchid for two weeks before he put his plan into action. This was as long as he dared risk--he did not wish to weaken the beast--merely to whet its appetite, that the outcome of the encounter might be more certain. And so, when he had carried the teacups back into the kitchen and was sitting upwind of Aunt Henrietta's cigar, he said casually: "I've got something I'd like to show you, Auntie. I've been keeping it as a surprise. It'll tickle you to death." That, he thought, was not a completely accurate description, but it gave the general idea.

Auntie took the cigar out of her mouth and looked at Hercules with frank surprise. "Well!" she boomed. "Wonders will never cease! What have you been up to, you rascal?" She slapped him playfully on the back and shot all the air out of his lungs. "You'll never believe it," gritted Hercules, when he had recovered his breath. "It's in the conservatory."

"Eh?" said Auntie, obviously puzzled.

"Yes--come along and have a look. It's going to create a real sensation." Auntie gave a snort that might have indicated disbelief, but followed Hercules without further question. The two Alsatians now busily chewing up the carpet looked at her anxiously and half rose to their feet, but she waved them away.

"All right, boys," she ordered gruffly. "I'll be back in a minute." Hercules thought this unlikely.

It was a dark evening, and the lights in the conservatory were off. As they entered, Auntie snorted, "Gad, Hercules--the place smells like a slaughterhouse. Haven't met such a stink since I shot that elephant in Bulawayo and we couldn't find it for a week." "Sorry, Auntie," apologised Hercules, propelling her forward through the gloom.

"It's a new fertiliser I'm using. It produces the most stunning results. Go on--another couple of yards. I want this to be a real surprise."

"I hope this isn't a joke," said Auntie suspiciously, as she stomped forward. "I can promise you it's no joke," replied Hercules, standing with his hand on the light switch. He could just see the loom- ing bulk of the orchid: Auntie was now within ten feet of it. He waited until she was well inside the danger zone, an threw the switch. There was a frozen moment while the scene was transfixed with light. Then Aunt Henrietta ground to a halt and stood, arms akimbo, in front of the giant orchid. For a moment Hercules was afraid she would retreat before the plant could go into action: then he saw that she was calmly scrutinising it, unable to make up her mind what the devil it was.

It was a full five seconds before the orchid moved. The the dangling tentacles flashed into action--but not in the way that Hercules had expected. The plant clutched them tighty, protectively, around itself--and at the same time it gave high-pitched scream of pure terror. In a moment of sickening disillusionment, Hercules realised the awful truth.

His orchid was an utter coward. It might be able to cope with the wild life of the Amazon jungle, but coming suddenlly upon Aunt Henrietta had completely broken its nerve.

As for its proposed victim, she stood watching the creature with an astonishment which swiftly changed to another emotion. She spun around on her heels and pointed an accusing finger at her nephew.

"Hercules!" she roared. "The poor thing's scared to death! Have you been bullying it?"

Hercules could only stand with his head hanging low in shame and frustration. "N-no, Auntie," he quavered. "I guess it's naturally nervous." "Well, I'm used to animals. You should have called me before. You must treat them firmly--but gently. Kindness al ways works, as long as you show them you're the master. There, there, did-dums--don't be frightened of Auntie--shi won't hurt you..." It was, thought Hercules in his blank despair, a revolting sight. With surprising gentleness, Aunt Henrietta fussed over the beast, patting and stroking it until the tentacles relax and the shrill, whistling scream died away. After a few min- utes of this pandering, it appeared to get over its fright. Hercules finally fled with a muffled sob when one of the tentacles crept forward and began to stroke Henrietta's gnarled fingers....

From that day, he was a broken man. What was worse, he could never escape from the consequences of his intended crime. Henrietta had acquired a new pet, and was liable to call not only at weekends but two or three times in between as well. It was obvious that she did not trust Hercules to treat the orchid properly, and still suspected him of bullying it. She would bring tasty tidbits that even her dogs had rejected, but which the orchid accepted with delight. The smell, which had so far been confined to the conservatory, began to creep into the house....

And there, concluded Harry Purvis, as he brought this improbable narrative to a close, the matter rests--to the satisfaction of two, at any rate, of the parties concerned. The orchid is happy, and Aunt Henrietta has something (query, someone?) else to dominate. From time to time the creature has a nervous breakdown when a mouse gets loose in the conservatory, and she rushes to console it.

As for Hercules, there is no chance that he will ever give any more trouble to either of them. He seems to have sunk into a kind of vegetable sloth: indeed, said Harry thoughtfully, every day he becomes more and more like an orchid himself. The harmless variety, of course....

Second Dawn

Complete Novelet Of Worlds Beyond

The aftermath of victory was terrible, but even worse was the realization that there must be more wars, unless the necessity could be removed...

Notes

"HERE THEY come," said Eris, rising to his fore-feet and turning to look down the long valley. For a moment the pain and bitterness had left his thoughts, so the even Jeryl, whose mind was more closely tuned to his than to any other, could scarcely detect it. There was even an undertone of softness that recalled poignantly the Eris she had known in the days before the War—the old Eris who now seemed almost as remote and as lost as if he were lying with all the others out there on the plain.

A dark tide was flowing up the valley, advancing with a curious hesitant motion, making odd pauses and little bounds forward. It was flanked with gold—the thin line of the Atheleni guards, so terrifyingly few compared with the black mass of the prisoners. But they were enough: indeed, they were only needed to guide that aimless river on its faltering way. Yet at the sight of so many thousands of the enemy, Jeryl found herself trembling; instinctively, she moved towards her mate, silver pelt resting against gold. Eris gave no sign that he had understood or even noticed the action.

The fear vanished as Jeryl saw how slowly the dark flood was moving forwards. She had been told what to expect, but the reality was even worse than she had imagined. As the prisoners came nearer, all the hate and bitterness ebbed from her mind, to be replaced by a sick compassion. No one of her race evermore need fear the aimless, idiot hoard that was being shepherded through the pass into the valley it would never leave again.

The guards were doing little more than urge the prisoners on with meaningless but encouraging cries, like nurses calling to infants too young to sense their thoughts. Strain as she might, Jeryl could detect no vestige of reason in any of those thousands of minds passing so near at hand. That brought home to her, more vividly than could anything else, the magnitude of the victory and of the defeat. Her mind was sensitive enough to detect the first faint thoughts of children, hovering on the verge of consciousness. The defeated enemy had become not even children, but babies with the bodies of adults.

The tide was passing within a few feet of them now. For the first time, Jeryl realized how much larger than her own people the Mithraneans were, and how beautifully the light of the twin suns gleamed on the dark satin of their bodies. Once a magnificent specimen, towering a full head above Eris, broke loose from the main body and came blundering towards them, halting a few paces away. Then it crouched down like a lost and frightened child, the splendid head moving uncertainly from side to side as if seeking it knew not what. For a moment the great, empty eyes fell full upon Jeryl's face. She was as beautiful, she knew, to the Mithraneans as to her own race—but there was no flicker of emotion on the blank features, and no pause in the aimless movement of the questing head. Then an exasperated guard drove the prisoner back to his fellows.

"Come away," Jeryl pleaded. "I don't want to see any more. Why did you ever bring me here?" The last thought was heavy with reproach.

Eris began to move away over the grassy slopes in great bounds that she could not hope to match, but as he went his mind threw its message back to hers. His thoughts were still gentle, though the pain beneath them was too deep to be concealed.

"I wanted everyone—even you—to see what we had to do to win the War. Then, perhaps, we will have no more in our lifetimes."

HE WAS waiting for her on the brow of the hill undistressed by the mad violence of his climb. The stream of prisoners was now too far below for them to see the details of its painful progress. Jeryl crouched down beside Eris and began to browse on the sparse vegetation that had been exiled from the fertile valley. She was slowly beginning to recover from the shock. "But what will happen to them?" she asked presently, still haunted by the memory of that splendid, mindless giant going into a captivity it could never understand.

"They can be taught how to eat," said Eris. "There is food in the valley for half a year, and then we'll move them on. It will be a heavy strain on our own resources, but we're under a moral obligation—and we've put it in the peace treaty."

"They can never be cured?"

"No. Their minds have been destroyed; they'll be like this until they die."

There was a long silence. Jeryl let her gaze wander across the hills, falling in gentle undulations to the edge of the ocean. She could just make out, beyond a gap in the hills, the distant line of blue that marked the sea—the mysterious, impassible sea. Its blue would soon be deepening into darkness, for the fierce white sun was setting; presently there would only be the red disc—hundreds of times larger but giving far less light—of its pale companion.

"I suppose we had to do it," Jeryl said at last. She was thinking almost to herself, but she let enough of her thoughts escape for Eris to overhear.

"You've seen them," he answered briefly. "They were bigger and stronger than we. Though we outnumbered them, it was stalemate: in the end, I think they would have won. By doing what we did, we saved thousands from death—or mutilation."

The bitterness came back into his thoughts, and Jeryl dared not look at him. He had screened the depths of his mind, but she knew that he was thinking of the shattered ivory stump upon his forehead. The War had been fought, except at the very end, with two weapons only—the razor-sharp hooves of the little, almost useless forepaws, and the splendid frontal horn that was the chief pride of every male. With this, Eris could never fight again, and from the loss stemmed much of the embittered harshness that sometimes made him hurt even those who loved him.

Eris was waiting for someone, though who it was Jeryl could not guess. She knew better than to interrupt his thoughts while he was in his present mood, and so remained silently beside him, her shadow merging with his as it stretched far along the hill-top.

Jeryl and Eris came of a race which, in Nature's lottery, had been luckier than most—and yet had missed one of the greatest prizes of all. They had powerful bodies and powerful minds, and they lived in a world which was both temperate and fertile. By human standards, they would have seemed strange, but by no means repulsive. Their sleek, fur-covered bodies tapered to a single giant rear-limb that could send them leaping over the ground in thirty-foot bounds. The two fore-limbs were much smaller, and served merely for support and steadying. They ended in pointed hooves that could be deadly in combat, but had no other useful purpose.

Both the Atheleni and their cousins, the Mithraneans, possessed mental powers that had enabled them to develop a very advanced mathematics and philosophy: but over the physical world they had no control at all. Houses, tools, clothes—indeed artifacts of any kind—were utterly unknown to them. To races which possessed hands, tentacles or other means of manipulation, their culture would have seemed incredibly limited: yet such is the adaptability of the mind, and the power of the commonplace, that they seldom realised their handicaps and could imagine no other way of life. It was natural to wander in great herds over the fertile plains, pausing where food was plentiful and moving on again when it was exhausted. This nomadic life had given them enough leisure for philosophy and even for certain arts. Their telepathic powers had not yet robbed them of their voices and they had developed a complex vocal music and an even more complex choreography. But they took the greatest pride of all in the range of their thoughts: for thousands of generations they had sent their minds roving through the misty infinities of metaphysics. Of physics, and indeed of all the sciences

of matter, they knew nothing—not even that they existed,
"Someone's coming," said Jeryl suddenly. "Who is it?"
Eris did not bother to look, but there was a sense of strain in his
reply.

"It's Aretenon. I agreed to meet him here."

"I'm so glad. You were such good friends once—it upset me when
you quarrelled."

Eris pawed fretfully at the turf, as he did when he was embarrassed
or annoyed. "I lost my temper with him when he left me during the
fifth battle of the Plain. Of course, I didn't know then why he had to
go."

Jeryl's eyes widened in sudden amazement and understanding. "You
mean—he had something to do with the Madness, and the way the
War ended?"

"Yes. There were very few people who knew more about the mind
than he did. I don't know what part he played, but it must have been
an important one. I don't suppose he'll ever be able to tell us much
about it."

STILL A considerable distance below them, Aretenon was zig-
zagging up the hillside in great leaps. A little later he had reached
them, and instinctively bent his head to touch horns with Eris in the
universal gesture of greeting. Then he stopped, horribly
embarrassed; there was an awkward pause until Jeryl came to the
rescue with some conventional remarks.

When Eris spoke, Jeryl was relieved to sense his obvious pleasure at
meeting his friend again, for the first time since their angry parting at
the height of the War. It had been longer still since her last meeting
with Aretenon, and she was surprised to see how much he had
changed. He was considerably younger than Eris—but no one would
have guessed it now. Some of his once-golden pelt was turning black
with age, and with a flash of his old humour Eris remarked that soon
no one would be able to tell him from a Mithranean.

Aretenon smiled. "That would have been useful in the last few weeks. I've just come through their country, helping to round up the Wanderers. We weren't very popular, as you might expect. If they'd known who I was, I don't suppose I'd have got back alive—armistice or no armistice."

"You weren't actually in charge of the Madness, were you?" asked Jeryl, unable to control her curiosity.

She had a momentary impression of thick, defensive mists forming around Aretenon's mind, shielding all his thoughts from the outer world. Then the reply came, curiously muffled, and with a sense of distance that was very rare in telepathic contact. "No: I wasn't in supreme charge. But there were only two others between myself and—the top."

"Of course," said Eris, rather petulantly, "I'm only an ordinary soldier and don't understand these things. But I'd like to know just how you did it. Naturally," he added, "neither Jeryl nor myself would talk to anyone else."

Again that veil seemed to descend over Aretenon's thoughts. Then it lifted, ever so slightly. "There's very little I'm allowed to tell. As you know, Eris, I was always interested in the mind and its workings. Do you remember the games we used to play, when I tried to uncover your thoughts, and you did your best to stop me? And how I sometimes made you carry out acts against your will?"

"I still think," said Eris, "that you couldn't have done that to a stranger, and that I was really unconsciously cooperating."

"That was true then—but it isn't any longer. The proof lies down there in the valley." He gestured towards the last stragglers who were being rounded up by the guards. The dark tide had almost passed, and soon the entrance to the valley would be closed.

"When I grew older," continued Aretenon, "I spent more and more of my time probing into the ways of the mind, and trying to discover why some of us can share our thoughts so easily, while others can never do so but must remain always isolated and alone, forced to

115

communicate by sounds or gestures. And I became fascinated by those rare minds that are completely deranged, so that those who possess them seem less than children.

"I had to abandon these studies when the War began. Then, as you know, they called for me one day during the fifth battle. Even now, I'm not quite sure who was responsible for that. I was taken to a place a long way from here, where I found a little group of thinkers many of whom I already knew.

"The plan was simple—and tremendous. From the dawn of our race we've known that two or three minds, linked together, could be used to control another mind if it was willing, in the way that I used to control you. We've employed this power for healing since ancient times. Now we planned to use it for destruction.

"There were two main difficulties. One was bound up with that curious limitation of our normal telepathic powers—the fact that, except in rare cases, we can only have contact over a distance with smmeone we already know, and can communicate with strangers only when we are actually in their presence.

"The second, and greater problem, was that the massed power of many minds would be needed, and never before had it been possible to link together more than two or three. How we succeeded is our main secret : like all such things, it seems easy now it has been done. And once we had started, it was simpler than we had expected. Two minds are more than twice as powerful as one, and three are much more than thrice as powerful as a single will. The exact mathematical relationship is an interesting one. You know how very rapidly the number of ways a group of objects may be arranged increases with the size of the group? Well, a similar relationship holds in this case.

"So in the end we had our Composite Mind. At first it was unstable, and we could only hold it together for a few seconds, It's still a tremendous strain on our mental resources, and even now we can only do it for—well, for long enough.

"All these experiments, of course, were carried out in great secrecy. If we could do this, so could the Mithraneans, for their minds are as good as ours. We had a number of their prisoners, and we used them as subjects."

FOR A MOMENT the veil that hid Aretenon's inner thoughts seemed to tremble and dissolve, then he regained control. "That was the worst part. It was bad enough to send madness into a far land, but it was infinitely worse when you could watch with your own eyes the effects of what you did.

"When we had perfected our technique, we made the first long-distance test. Our victim was someone so well-known to one of our prisoners—whose mind we had taken over—that we could identify him completely and thus the distance between us was no objection. The experiment worked, but of course no one suspected that we were responsible.

"We did not operate again until we were certain that our attack would be so overwhelming that it would end the War. From the minds of our prisoners we had identified about a score of Mithraneans—their friends and kindred—in such detail that we could pick them out and destroy them. As each mind fell beneath our attack, it gave up to us the knowledge of others, and so our power increased. We could have done far more damage than we did, for we took only the males."

"Was that," said Jeryl bitterly, "so very merciful?"

"Perhaps not: but it should be remembered to our credit. We stopped as soon as the enemy sued for peace; and, as we alone knew what had happened, we went into their country to undo what damage we could. It was little enough."

There was a long silence. The valley was deserted now, and the white sun had set. A cold wind was blowing over the hills, passing, where none could follow it, out across the empty and untravelled sea. Then Eris spoke, his thoughts almost whispering in Aretenon's mind. "You did not come to tell me this, did you? There is something more." It was a statement rather than a query.

"Yes," replied Aretenon. "I have a message for you—one that will surprise you a good deal. It's from Therodimus."

"Therodimus! I thought—"

"You thought he was dead or worse still, a traitor. He's neither, although he's lived in enemy territory for the last twenty years. The Mithraneans treated him as we did, and gave him everything he needed. They recognized his mind for what it was, and even during the War no one touched him. Now he wants to see you again."

WHATEVER emotions Eris was feeling at this news of his old teacher, he gave no sign of them. Perhaps he was recalling his youth, remembering now that Therodimus had played a greater part in the shaping of his mind than any other single influence. But his thoughts were barred to Aretenon and even to Jeryl.

"What's he been doing all this time?" Eris asked at length. "And why does he want to see me now?"

"It's a long and complicated story," said Aretenon, "but Therodimus has made a discovery quite as remarkable as ours, and one that may have even greater consequences."

"Discovery? What sort of discovery?"

Aretenon paused, looking thoughtfully along the valley. The guards were returning, leaving behind only the few who would be needed to deal with any wandering prisoners.

"You know as much of our history as I do, Eris," he began. "It took, we believe, something like a million generations for us to reach our present level of development—and that's a tremendous length of time! Almost all the progress we've made has been due to our telepathic powers: without them we'd be little different from all those other animals that show such puzzling resemblances to us. We're very proud of our philosophy and our mathematics, of our music and dancing—but have you ever thought, Eris, that there might be other lines of cultural development which we've never even dreamed of? That there might be other forces in the Universe besides mental ones?"

"I don't know what you mean," said Eris flatly.

"It's hard to explain, and I won't try—except to say this. Do you realise just how pitiably feeble is our control over the external world, and how useless these limbs of ours really are? No—you can't, for you won't have seen what I have. But perhaps this will make you understand."

The pattern of Aretenon's thoughts modulated suddenly into a minor key. "I remember once coming upon a bank of beautiful and curiously complicated flowers. I wanted to see what they were like inside, so I tried to open one, steadying it between my hooves and picking it apart with my teeth. I tried again and again—and failed. In the end, half mad with rage, I trampled all those flowers into the dirt."

Jeryl could detect the perplexity in Eris' mind, but she could see that he was interested and curious to know more.

"I have had that sort of feeling, too," he admitted. "But what can one do about it? And after all, is it really important? There are a good many things in this universe which are not exactly as we should like them."

Aretenon smiled. "That's true enough. But Therodimus has found how to do something about it. Will you come and see him?"

"It must be a long journey."

"About twenty days from here, and we have to go across a river."

Jeryl felt Eris give a little shudder. The Atheleni hated water, for the excellent and sufficient reason that they were too heavily-boned to swim, and promptly drowned if they fell into it.

"It's in enemy territory: they won't like me."
"They respect you, and it might be a good idea for you to go—a friendly gesture, as it were."

"But I'm wanted here."

"You can take my word that nothing you do here is as important as the message Therodimus has for you—and for the whole world."

Eris veiled his thoughts for a moment, then uncovered them briefly.

"I'll think about it," he said.

IT WAS surprising how little Aretenon managed to say on the many days of the journey. From time to time Eris would challenge the defences of his mind with half-playful thrusts, but always they were parried with an effortless skill. About the ultimate weapon that had ended the War he would say nothing, but Eris knew that those who had wielded it had not yet disbanded and were still at their secret hiding place. Yet, though he would not talk about the past, Aretenon often spoke of the future, with the urgent anxiety of one who had helped shape it and was not sure if he had acted aright. Like many others of his race, he was haunted by what he had done; the sense of guilt sometimes overwhelmed him. Often he made remarks which puzzled Eris at the time, but which he was to remember more and more vividly in the years ahead.

"We've come to a turning-point in our history, Eris. The powers we've uncovered will soon be shared by the Mithraneans, and another war will mean destruction for us both. All my life I've worked to increase our knowledge of the mind; but now I wonder if I've brought something into the world that is too powerful, and too dangerous, for us to handle. Yet—it's too late, now, to retrace our footsteps: sooner or later our culture was bound to come to this point, and to discover what we hava found.

"It's a terrible dilemma and there's only one solution. We cannot go back, and if we go forward we may meet disaster. So we must change the very nature of our civilisation, and break completely with the million generations behind us. You can't imagine how that could be done: nor could I, until I met Therodimus and he told me of his dream.

"The mind is a wonderful thing, Eris—but by itself it is helpless in the universe of matter. We know now how to multiply the power of our brains by an enormous factor: we can solve, perhaps, the great problems of mathematics that have baffled us for ages. But neither our unaided minds, nor the group-mind we've now created, can alter in the slightest the one fact that all through history has brought us and the Mithraneans into conflict—the fact that the food supply is fixed and our populations are not." Jeryl would watch them, taking little part in their thoughts, as they argued these matters, Most of their discussions took place while they were browsing, for like all active ruminants they had to spend a considerable part of each day searching for food. Fortunately, the land through which they were passing was extremely fertile—indeed, its fertility had been one of the causes of the War. Eris, Jeryl was glad to see, was becoming something of his old self again. The feeling of frustrated bitterness that had filled his mind for so many months had not lifted, but it was no longer as all-pervading as it had been.

THEY LEFT the open plain on the twenty-second day of their journey. For a long time they had been travelling through Mithranean territory, but those few of their ex-enemies they had seen had been inquisitive rather than hostile. Now the grasslands were coming to an end, and the forest with all its primeval terrors lay ahead.

"Only one carnivore lives in this region," Aretenon reassured them, "and it's no match for the three of us. We'll be past the trees in a day and a night."

"A night—in the forest!" gasped Jeryl, half petrified with terror at the very thought.

Aretenon was obviously a little ashamed of himself. "I didn't like to mention it before," he apologised, "but there's really no danger. I've done it by myself, several times. After all, none of the great flesh-eaters of ancient times still exists—and it won't be really dark, even in the woods. The red sun will still be up."

Jeryl was still trembling slightly. She came of a race which, for thousands of generations, had lived on the high hills and the open plains, relying on speed to escape from danger. The thought of going

121

among trees—and in the dim red twilight while the primary sun was down—filled her with panic. And of the three of them, only Aretenon possessed a horn with which to fight. (It was nothing like so long or sharp, thought Jeryl, as Eris' had been.)

She was still not at all happy, even when they had spent a completely uneventful day moving through the woods. The only animals they saw were tiny, long-tailed creatures that ran up and down the tree trunks with amazing speed, gibbering with anger as the intruders passed. It was entertaining to watch them, but Jeryl did not think that the forest would be quite so amusing in the night.

Her fears were well founded. When the fierce white sun passed below the trees, and the crimson shadows of the red giant lay everywhere, a change seemed to come over the world. A sudden silence swept across the forest—a silence abruptly broken by a very distant wail towards which the three of them turned instinctively, ancestral warnings shrieking in their minds.

"What was that?" gasped Jeryl.

Aretenon was breathing swiftly, but his reply was calm enough. "Never mind," he said. "It was a long way off. I don't know what it was."

And Jeryl knew that he was lying.

They took turns to keep guard, and the long night wore slowly away. From time to time Jeryl would awaken from troubled dreams into the nightmare reality of the strange, distorted trees gathered threateningly around her. Once, when she was on guard, she heard the sound of a heavy body moving through the woods very far away—but it came no nearer and she did not disturb the others. So at last the longed-for brillance of the white sun began to flood the sky, and the day had come again.

Aretenon, Jeryl thought, was probably more relieved than he pretended to be. He was almost boyish as he frisked around in the morning sunlight, snatching an occasional mouthful of foliage from an overhanging branch.

"We've only half a day to go now," he said cheerfully. "We'll be out of the forest by noon."

There was a mischievous undertone to his thoughts that puzzled Jeryl. It seemed as if Aretenon was keeping still another secret from them, and Jeryl wondered what further obstacles they would have to overcome. By midday she knew, for their way was barred by a great river flowing slowly past them as if in no haste to meet the sea.

Eris looked at it with some annoyance, measuring it with a practised eye. "It's much too deep to ford here. We'll have to go a long way upstream before we can cross."

Aretenon smiled. "On the contrary," he said cheerfully, "we're going downstream."

Eris and Jeryl looked at him in amazement.

"Are you mad?" Eris cried.

"You'll soon see. We've not far to go now—you've come all this way, so you might as well trust me for the rest of the journey."

THE RIVER slowly widened and deepened. If it had been impassable before, it was doubly so now. Sometimes, Eris knew, one came upon a stream across which a tree had fallen, so that one could walk over on the trunk—though it was a risky thing to do. But this river was the width of many trees, and was growing no narrower.

"We're nearly there," said Aretenon at last. "I recognize the place. Someone should be coming out of those woods at any moment." He gestured with his horn to the trees on the far side of the river, and almost as he did so three figures came bounding out on to the bank. Two of them, Jeryi saw, were Atheleni: the third was a Mithranean.

They were now nearing a great tree, standing by the water's edge, but Jeryl had paid it little attention: she was too interested in the figures on the distant bank, wondering what they were going to do next. So when Eris' amazement exploded like a thunderclap in the depths of her own mind, she was too confused for a moment to realise its cause. Then she turned towards the tree, and saw what Eris had seen.

To some minds and some races, few things could have been more natural or more commonplace than a thick rope tied round a tree trunk, and floating out across the waters of a river to another tree on the far bank. Yet it filled both Jeryl and Eris with the terror of the unknown, and for one awful moment Jeryl thought that a gigantic snake was emerging from the water. Then she saw that it was not alive, but her fear remained. For it was the first artificial object that she had ever seen.

"Don't worry about what it is, or how it was put there," counselled Aretenon. "It's going to carry you across, and that's all that matters for the moment. Look—there's someone coming over now!"

One of the figures on the far bank had lowered itself into the water, and was working its way with its forelimbs along the rope. As it came nearer—it was the Mithranean, and a female—Jeryl saw that it was carrying a second and much smaller rope looped round the upper part of its body.

With the skill of long practice, the stranger made her way across the floating cable, and emerged dripping from the river. She seemed to know Aretenon, but Jeryl could not intercept their thoughts.

"I can go across without any help," said Aretenon, "but I'll show you the easy way."

He slipped the loop over his shoulders, and, dropping into the water, hooked his fore-limbs over the fixed cable. A moment later he was being dragged across at a great speed by the two others on the far bank, where, after much trepidation, Eris and Jeryl presently joined him.

It was not the sort of bridge one would expect from a race which could quite easily have dealt with the mathematics of a reinforced concrete arch—if the possibility of such an object had ever occurred to it. But it served its purpose, and once it had been made, they could use it rapidly enough.

Once it had been made. But—who had made it?

WHEN their dripping guides had rejoined them, Aretenon gave his friends a warning. "I'm afraid you're going to have a good many shocks while you're here. You'll see some very strange sights, but when you understand them, they'll cease to puzzle you in the slightest. In fact, you will soon come to take them for granted."

One of the strangers, whose thoughts neither Eris nor Jeryl could intercept, was giving him a message.

"Therodimus is waiting for us," said Aretenon. "He's very anxious to see you."

"I've been trying to contact him," complained Eris, "but I've not succeeded."

Aretenon seemed a little troubled. "You'll find he's changed," he said. "And after all, you've not seen each other for many years. It may be some time before you can make full contact again."

Their road was a winding one through the forest, and from time to time curiously narrow paths branched off in various directions. Therodimus, thought Eris, must have changed indeed for him to have taken up permanent residence among trees. Presently the track opened out into a large, semi-circular clearing with a low white cliff lying along its diameter. At the foot of the cliff were several dark holes of varying sizes—obviously the openings of caves.

It was the first time that either Eris or Jeryl had ever entered a cave, and they did not greatly look forward to the experience. They were relieved when Aretenon told them to wait just outside the opening, and went on alone towards the puzzling yellow light that glowed in the depths. A moment later, dim memories began to pulse in Eris' mind, and he knew that his old teacher was coming, even though he could no longer fully share his thoughts.

Something stirred in the gloom, and then Therodimus came out into the sunlight. At the sight of him, Jeryl screamed once and buried her head in Eris' mane, but Eris stood firm, though he was trembling as he had never done before battle. For Therodimus blazed with a magnificence that none of his race had ever known since history began. Around his neck hung a band of glittering objects that caught and refracted the sunlight in a myriad colours, while covering his body was a sheet of some thick, many-hued material that rustled softly as he walked. And his horn was no longer the yellow of ivory: some magic had changed it to the most wonderful purple that Jeryl had ever seen.

Therodimus stood motionless for a moment, savouring their amazement to the full. Then his rich laugh echoed in their minds, and he reared up upon his hind limb. The coloured garment fell whispering to the ground, and at a toss of his head the glittering necklace arced like a rainbow into a corner of the cave. But the purple horn remained unchanged.

It seemed to Eris that he stood at the brink of a great chasm, with Therodimus beckoning to him on the far side. Their thoughts struggled to form a bridge, but could make no contact. Between them was the gulf of half a lifetime and many battles, of a myriad unshared experiences—Therodimus' years in this strange land, his own mating with Jeryl and the memory of their lost children. Though they stood face to face, a few feet only between them, their thoughts could never meet again.

Then Aretenon, with all the power and authority of his unsurpassed skill, did something to his mind that Eris was never quite able to recall. He only knew that the years seemed to have rolled back, that he was once more the eager, anxious pupil—and that he could speak to Therodimus again.

IT WAS strange to sleep underground, but less unpleasant than spending the night amid the unknown terrors of the forest. As she watched the crimson shadows deepening beyond the entrance of the little cave, Jeryl tried to collect her scattered thoughts. She had understood only a small part of what had passed between Eris and Therodimus, but she knew that something incredible was taking place. The evidence of her eyes was enough to prove that: today she had seen things for which there were no words in her language.

She had heard things, too. As they had passed one of the cave-mouths, there had come from it a rhythmic, "whirring" sound, unlike that made by any animal she knew. It had continued steadily without pause or break as long as she could hear it, and even now its unhurried rhythm had not left her mind. Aretenon, she believed, had also noticed it, though without any surprise: Eris had been too engrossed with Therodimus.

The old philosopher had told them very little, preferring, as he said, to show them his empire when they had had a good night's rest. Nearly all their talk had been concerned with the events of their own land during the last few years, and Jeryl found it somewhat boring. Only one thing had interested her, and she had eyes for little else. That was the wonderful chain of coloured crystals that Therodimus had worn around his neck. What it was, or how it had been created, she could not imagine: but she coveted it. As she fell asleep, she found herself thinking idly, but more than half seriously, of the sensation it would cause if she returned to her people with such a marvel gleaming against her own pelt. It would look so much better there than upon old Therodimus.

Aretenon and Therodimus met them at the cave soon after dawn. The philosopher had discarded his regalia—which he had obviously worn only to impress his guests—and his horn had returned to its normal yellow. That was one thing Jeryl thought she could understand, for she had come across fruits whose juices could cause such colour changes.

Therodimus settled himself at the mouth of the cave. He began his narration without any preliminaries, and Eris guessed that he must have told it many times before to earlier visitors.
"I came to this place, Eris, about five years after leaving our country. As you know, I was always interested in strange lands, and from the Mithraneans I'd heard rumours that intrigued me very much. How I traced them to their source is a long story that doesn't matter now. I crossed the river far up-stream one summer, when the water was very low. There's only one place where it can be done, and then only

in the driest years. Higher still the river loses itself in the mountains, and I don't think there's any way through them. So this is virtually an island—almost completely cut off from Mithranean territory.

"It's an island, but it's not uninhabited. The people who live here are called the Phileni, and they have a very remarkable culture—one entirely different from our own. Some of the products of the culture you've already seen.

"As you know, there are many different races on our world, and quite a few of them have some sort of intelligence. But there is a great gulf between us and all other creatures. As far as we know, we are the only beings capable of abstract thought and complex logical processes.

"The Phileni are a much younger race than ours, and they are intermediate between us and the other animals. They've lived here on this rather large island for several thousand generations—but their rate of development has been many, many times swifter than ours. They neither possess nor understand our telepathic powers, but they have something else which we may well envy—something which is responsible for the whole of their civilization and its incredibly rapid progress."

Therodimus paused, then rose slowly to his feet.

"Follow me," he said. "I'll take you to see the Phileni."

HE LED them back to the caves from which they had come the night before, pausing at the entrance from which Jeryl had heard that strange, rhythmic whirring. It was clearer and louder now, and she saw Eris start as though he had noticed it for the first time. Then Therodimus uttered a high-pitched whistle, and at once the whirring slackened, falling octave by octave until it had ebbed into silence. A moment later something came towards them out of the semi-gloom.

It was a little creature, scarcely half their height, and it did not hop, but walked upon two jointed limbs that seemed very thin and feeble. Its large spherical head was dominated by three huge eyes, set far apart and capable of independent movement. With the best will in the world, Jeryl did not think it was very attractive.

Then Therodimus uttered another whistle, and the creature raised its fore-limbs towards them.

"Look closely," said Therodimus, very gently, "and you will see the answer to many of your questions."

For the first time, Jeryl saw that the creature's fore-limbs did not end in hooves, or indeed after the fashion of any animal with which she was acquainted. Instead, they divided into at least a dozen thin, flexible tentacles and two hooked claws.

"Go towards it, Jeryl," commanded Therodimus. "It has something for you."

Hesitantly, Jeryl moved forward. She noticed that the creature's body was crossed with bands of some dark material, to which were attached unidentifiable objects. It dropped a fore-limb to one of these, and a cover opened to reveal a cavity inside which something glittered. Then the little tentacles were clutching that marvellous crystal necklace, and with a movement so swift and dexterous that Jeryl could scarcely follow it, the Phileni moved forward and clasped it round her neck.

Therodimus brushed aside her confusion and gratitude, but his shrewd old mind was well pleased. Jeryl would be his ally now in whatever he planned to do. But Eris' emotions might not be so easily swayed, and in this matter mere logic was not enough. His old pupil had changed so much, had been so deeply wounded by the past, that Therodimus could not be certain of success. Yet he had a plan that could turn even these difficulties to his advantage.

He gave another whistle, and the Phileni made a curious waving gesture with its hands and disappeared into the cave. A moment later that strange whirring ascended once more from the silence, but Jeryl's curiosity was now quite overshadowed by her delight in her new possession.

"We'll go through the woods," said Therodimus, "to the nearest settlement—it's only a little way from here. The Phileni don't live in the open, as we do. In fact, they differ from us in almost every conceivable way. I'm even afraid," he added ruefully, "that they're much better-natured than we are, and I believe that one day they'll be more intelligent. But first of all, let me tell you what I've learned about them, so that you can understand what I'm planning to do."

The mental evolution of any race is conditioned, even dominated, by physical factors which that race almost invariably takes for granted as part of the natural order of things. The wonderfully sensitive hands of the Phileni had enabled them to find by experiment and trial facts which had taken the planet's only other intelligent species a thousand times as long to discover by pure deduction. Quite early in their history, the Phileni had invented simple tools. From these they had proceeded to fabrics, pottery, and the use of fire. When Therodimus had discovered them, they had already invented the lathe and the potter's wheel, and were about to move into their first Metal Age with all that that implied.

On the purely intellectual plane, their progress had been less rapid. They were clever and skillful, but they had a dislike of abstract thought and their mathematics was purely empirical. They knew, for example, that a triangle with sides in the ratio three-four-five was right-angled, but had not suspected that this was only a special case of a much more general law. Their knowledge was full of such yawning gaps, which despite the help of Therodimus and his several score disciples, they seemed in no great hurry to fill.

Therodimus they worshipped as a god, and for two whole generations of their short-lived race they had obeyed him in everything, giving him all the products of their skill that he needed, and making at his suggestion the new tools and devices that had occurred to him. The partnership had been incredibly fertile, for it was as if both races had suddenly been released from their shackles. Great manual skill and greater intellectual powers had fused in a fruitful union probably unique in all the universe—and progress that would normally have taken millenia had been achieved in less than a decade.

AS ARETENON had promised them, though Eris and Jeryl saw many marvels, they came across nothing that they could not understand once they had watched the little Phileni craftsmen at work and had seen with what magic their hands shaped natural materials into lovely or useful forms. Even their tiny towns and primitive farms soon lost their wonder and became part of the accepted order of things.

Therodimus let them look their fill, until they had seen every aspect of this strangely sophisticated stone-age culture. Because they knew no differently, they found nothing incongruous in the sight of a Phileni potter—who could scarcely count beyond ten—shaping a series of complex algebraic surfaces under the guidance of a young Mithranean mathematician. Like all his race, Eris possessed tremendous powers of mental visualization, but he realized how much easier geometry would be if one could actually see the shapes one was considering. From this beginning (though he could not guess it) would one day evolve the idea of a written language.

Jeryl was fascinated above all things by the sight of the little Phileni women weaving fabrics upon their primitive looms. She could sit for hours watching the flying shuttles and wishing that she could use them. Once one had seen it done, it seemed so simple and so obvious—and so utterly beyond the power of the clumsy, useless limbs of her own people.

They grew very fond of the Phileni, who seemed eager to please and were pathetically proud of all their manual skills. In these new and novel surroundings, meeting fresh wonders every day, Eris seemed to be recovering from some of the scars which the War had left upon his mind. Jeryl knew, however, that there was still much damage to be undone. Sometimes, before he could hide them, she would come across raw, angry wounds in the depths of Eris' mind, and she feared that many of them—like the broken stump of his horn—would never heal. Eris had hated the War, and the manner of its ending still oppressed him. Beyond this, Jeryl knew, he was haunted by the fear that it might come again.

These troubles she often discussed with Therodimus, of whom she had now grown very fond. She still did not fully understand why he had brought them here, or what he and his followers were planning to do. Therodimus was in no hurry to explain his actions, for he wished Jeryl and Eris to draw their own conclusions as far as possible. But at last, five days after their arrival, he called them to his cave.

"You've now seen," he began, "most of the things we have to show you here. You know what the Phileni can do, and perhaps you have thought how much our own lives will be enriched once we can use the products of their skill. That was my first thought when I came here, all those years ago."

"It was an obvious and rather naive idea, but it led to a much greater one. As I grew to know the Phileni, and found how swiftly their minds had advanced in so short a time, I realized what a fearful disadvantage our own race had always laboured under. I began to wonder how much further forward we would have been had we the Phileni's control over the physical world. It is not a question of mere convenience, or the ability to make beautiful things like that necklace of yours, Jeryl, but something much more profound. It is the difference between ignorance and knowledge, between weakness and power."

"We have developed our minds, and our minds alone, until we can go no further. As Aretenon has told you, we have now come to a danger that threatens our entire race. We are under the shadow of the irresistible weapon against which there can be no defense.

"The solution is, quite literally, in the hands of the Phileni. We must use their skills to reshape our world, and so remove the cause of all our wars. We must go back to the beginning and re-lay the foundations of our culture. It won't be our culture alone, though, for we shall share it with the Phileni. They will be the hands—we the brains. Oh, I have dreamed of the world that may come, ages ahead, when even the marvels you see around you now will be considered childish toys! But not many are philosophers, and I need an argument more substantial than dreams. That final argument I believe I may have found, though I cannot yet be certain.

"I have asked you here, Eris, partly because I wanted to renew our old friendship, and partly because your word will now have far greater influence than mine. You are a hero among your own people, and the Mithraneans also will listen to you. I want you to return, taking with you some of the Phileni and their products. Show them to your people, and ask them to send their young men here to help us with our work."

There was a pause during which Jeryl could gather no hint of Eris' thoughts. Then he replied hesitantly: "But I still don't understand. These things that the Phileni make are very pretty, and some of them may be useful to us. But how can they change us as profoundly as you seem to think?"

Therodimus sighed. Eris could not see past the present into the future that was yet to be. He had not caught, as Therodimus had done, the promise that lay beyond the busy hands and tools of the Phileni—the first faint intimations of the Machine. Perhaps he would never understand: but he could still be convinced.

Veiling his deeper thoughts, Therodimus continued: "Perhaps some of these things are toys, Eris—but they may be more powerful than you think. Jeryl, I know, would be loath to part with hers...and perhaps I can find one that would convince you."

Eris was sceptical, and Jeryl could see that he was in one of his darker moods. "I doubt it very much," he said.

"Well, I can try." Therodimus gave a whistle, and one of the Phileni came running up. There was a short exchange of conversation.

"Would you come with me, Eris? It will take some time."

ERIS FOLLOWED him, the others, at Therodimus' request, remaining behind. They left the large cave and went towards the row of smaller ones which the Phileni used for their various trades.

The strange whirring was sounding loudly in Eris' ears, but for a moment he could not see its cause, the light of the crude oil lamps being too faint for his eyes. Then he made out one of the Phileni bending over a wooden table upon which something was spinning rapidly, driven by a belt from a treadle operated by another of the little creatures. He had seen the potters using a similar device, but this was different. It was shaping wood, not clay, and the potter's fingers had been replaced by a sharp metal blade from which long, thin shavings were curling out in fascinating spirals. With their huge eyes the Phileni, who disliked full sunlight, could see perfectly in the gloom, but it was some time before Eris could discover just what was happening, then suddenly he understood.

"Aretenon," said Jeryl when the others had left them, "why should the Phileni do all these things for us? Surely they're quite happy as they are?"

The question, Aretenon thought, was typical of Jeryl and would never have been asked by Eris.

"They will do anything that Therodimus says," he answered; "but even apart from that, there's so much we can give them as well. When we turn our minds to their problems, we can see how to solve them in ways that would never have occurred to them. They're very eager to learn, and already we must have advanced their culture by hundreds of generations. Also, they're physically very feeble. Although we don't possess their dexterity, our strength makes possible tasks they could never attempt."

They had wandered to the edge of the river, and stood for a moment watching the unhurried waters moving down to the sea. Then Jeryl turned to go upstream, but Aretenon stopped her.

"Therodimus doesn't want us to go that way, yet," he explained. "It's just another of his little secrets; he never likes to reveal his plans until they're ready."

Slightly piqued, and distinctly curious, Jeryl obediently turned back. She would, of course, come this way again as soon as there was no one else about.

It was very peaceful here in the warm sunlight, among the pools of heat trapped by the trees. Jeryl had almost lost her fear of the forests though she knew she would never be quite happy there.

Aretenon seemed very abstracted, and Jeryl knew that he wished to say something and was marshalling his thoughts. Presently he began to speak, with the freedom that is only possible between two people who are fond of each other but have no emotional ties.

"It is very hard, Jeryl," he began, "to turn one's back on the work of a lifetime. Once I had hoped that the great new forces we have discovered could be safely used, but now I know that is impossible, at least for many ages. Therodimus was right—we can go no further with our minds alone. Our culture has been hopelessly one-sided, though through no fault of ours. We cannot solve the fundamental problems of peace and war without a command over the physical world such as the Phileni possess—and which we hope to borrow from them.

"Perhaps there will be other great adventures here for our minds, to make us forget what we have had to abandon. We shall be able to learn something from Nature at last. What is the difference between fire and water, between wood and stone? What are the suns, and what are those millions of faint lights we see in the sky when both the suns are down? Perhaps the answers to all these questions may lie at the end of the new road along which we must travel."

He paused.
"New knowledge—new wisdom—in realms we have never dreamed of before. It may lure us away from the dangers we have encountered: for certainly nothing we can learn from Nature will ever be as great a threat as the peril we have uncovered in our own minds."

The flow of Aretenon's thoughts was suddenly interrupted. Then he said: "I think that Eris wants to see you."

Jeryl wondered why Eris had not sent the message to her: she wondered, too, at the undertone of amusement—or was it something else?—in Aretenon's mind.

THERE WAS no sign of Eris as they approached the caves, but he was waiting for them and came bounding out into the sunlight before they could reach the entrance. Then Jeryl gave an involuntary cry, and retreated a pace or two as her mate came towards her.

For Eris was whole again. Gone was the shattered stump on his forehead: it had been replaced by a new, gleaming horn no less splendid than the one that he had lost.

In a belated gesture of greeting, Eris touched horns with Aretenon. Then he was gone into the forest in great joyous leaps—but not before his mind had met Jeryl's as it had seldom done since the days before the War.

"Let him go," said Therodimus softly. "He would rather be alone. When he returns, I think you will find him—different." He gave a little laugh. "The Phileni are clever, are they not? Now, perhaps, Eris will be more appreciative of their 'toys'."

"I know I am impatient," said Therodimus, "but I am old now, and I want to see the changes begin in my own lifetime. That is why I am starting so many schemes in the hope that some at least will succeed. But this is the one, above all, in which I have put most faith."

For a moment he lost himself in his thoughts. Not one in a hundred of his own race could fully share his dream. Even Eris, though he now believed in it, did so with his heart rather than his mind. Perhaps Aretenon—the brilliant and subtle Aretenon, so desperately anxious to neutralize the powers he had brought into the world—might have glimpsed the reality. But his was of all minds the most impenetrable, save when he wished otherwise.

"You know as well as I do," continued Therodimus, as they walked upstream, "that our wars have only one cause—Food. We and the Mithraneans are trapped on this continent of ours with its limited resources, which we can do nothing to increase. Ahead of us we have always the nightmare of starvation, and for all our vaunted intelligence there has been nothing we can do about it. Oh yes, we have scraped some laborious irrigation ditches with our fore-hooves, but how slight their help has been!

136

"The Phileni have discovered how to grow crops that increase the fertility of the ground many-fold. I believe that we can do the same—once we have adapted their tools for our own use. That is our first and most important task, but it is not the one on which I have set my heart. The final solution to Our problem, Eris, must be the discovery of new, virgin lands into which our people can migrate"

He smiled at the other's amazement.

"No, don't think I'm mad. Such lands do exist, I'm sure of it. Once I stood at the edge of the ocean and watched a great flight of birds coming inland from far out at sea. I have seen them flying outwards, too, so purposefully that I was certain they were going to some other country. And I have followed them with my thoughts."

"Even if your theory is true, as it probably is," said Eris, "what use is it to us?" He gestured to the river flowing beside them. "We drown in the water, and you cannot build a rope to support us—" His thoughts suddenly faded out into a jumbled chaos of ideas.

Therodimus smiled. "So you have guessed what I hope to do. Well, now you can see if you are right."

They had come to a level stretch of bank, upon which a group of the Phileni were busily at work, under the supervision of some of Therodimus' assistants. Lying at the water's edge was a strange object which, Eris realized, was made of many tree-trunks joined together by ropes.

They watched in fascination as the orderly tumult reached its climax. There was a great pulling and pushing, and the raft moved ponderously into the water with a mighty splash. The spray had scarcely ceased to fall when a young Mithranean leaped from the bank and began to dance gleefully upon the logs, which were now tugging at the moorings as if eager to break away and follow the river down to the sea. A moment later he had been joined by others, rejoicing in their mastery of a new element. The little Phileni, unable to make the leap, stood watching patiently on the bank while their masters enjoyed themselves.

There was an exhilaration about the scene that no one could fail to miss, though perhaps few of those present realized that they were at a turning point in history. Only Therodimus stood a little apart from the rest, lost in his own thoughts. This primitive raft, he knew, was merely a beginning. It must be tested upon the river, then along the shores of the ocean. The work would take years, and he was never likely to see the first voyagers returning from those fabulous lands whose existence was still no more than a guess. But what had been begun, others would finish.

Overhead, a flight of birds was passing across the forest. Therodimus watched them go, envying their freedom to move at will over land and sea. He had begun the conquest of the water for his race, but that the skies might one day be theirs also was beyond even his imagination.

ARETENON, Jeryl and the rest of the expedition had already crossed the river when Eris said good-bye to Therodimus. This time they had done so without a drop of water touching their bodies, for the raft had come down-stream and was performing valuable duties as a ferry. A new and much improved model was already under construction, as it was painfully obvious that the prototype was not exactly seaworthy. These initial difficulties would be quickly overcome by designers who, even if they were forced to work with stone-age tools, could handle with ease the mathematics of metacenters, buoyancies and advanced hydrodynamics.
"Your task won't be a simple one," said Therodimus, "for you cannot show your people all the things you have seen here. At first you must be content to sow the seed, to arouse interest and curiosity—particularly among the young, who will come here to learn more. Perhaps you will meet opposition: I expect so. But every time you return to us, we shall have new things to show you and to strengthen your arguments."

They touched horns: then Eris was gone, taking with him the knowledge that was to change the world—so slowly at first, then ever more swiftly. Once the barriers were down, once the Mithraneans and the Atheleni had been given the simple tools which they could fasten to their fore-limbs and use unaided, progress would be swift. But for the present they must rely on the Phileni for everything: and there were so few of them.

Therodimus was well content. Only in one respect was he disappointed, for he had hoped that Eris, who had always been his favorite, might also be his successor. The Eris who was now returning to his own people was no longer self-obsessed or embittered, for he had a mission and hope for the future. But he lacked the keen, far-ranging vision that was needed here: it would be Aretenon who must continue what he had begun. Still, that could not be helped, and there was no need yet to think of such matters. Therodimus was very old, but he knew that he would be meeting Eris many times again here by the river at the entrance to his land.

THE FERRY was gone now, and though he had expected it, Eris stopped amazed at the great span of the bridge, swaying slightly in the breeze. Its execution did not quite match its design—a good deal of mathematics had gone into its parabolic suspension—but it was still the first great engineering feat in history. Constructed though it was entirely of wood and rope, it forecast the shape of the metal giants to come.

Eris paused in mid-stream. He could see smoke rising from the shipyards facing the ocean, and thought he could just glimpse the masts of some of the new vessels that were being built for coastal trade.

Aretenon was waiting for them on the far bank. He moved rather slowly now, but his eyes were still bright with the old, eager intelligence. He greeted Eris warmly. "I'm glad you could come now. You're just in time."

"The ships are back?"

"Almost: they were sighted an hour ago, out on the horizon. They should be here at any moment, and then we shall know the truth at last, after all these years. If only—"

His thoughts faded out, but Eris could continue them. They had come to the great pyramid of stones beneath which Therodimus lay—Therodimus, whose brain was behind everything they saw, but who could never learn now if his most cherished dream was true or not.

There was a storm coming up from the ocean, and they hurried along the new road that skirted the river's edge. Small boats of a kind that Eris had not seen before went past them occasionally, operated by Atheleni or Mithraneans with wooden paddles strapped to their forelimbs. It always gave Eris great pleasure to see such new conquests, such new liberations of his people from their age-old chains. Yet sometimes they reminded him of children who had suddenly been let loose into a wonderful new world, full of exciting and interesting things that must be done, whether they were likely to be useful or not. However, anything that promised to make his race into better sailors was more than useful. In the last decade Eris had discovered that pure intelligence was sometimes not enough: there were skills that could not be acquired by any amount of mental effort. Though his people had largely overcome their fear of water, they were still quite incompetent on the ocean, and the Phileni had therefore become the first navigators of the world.

Jeryl looked nervously around her as the first peal of thunder come rolling in from the sea. She was still wearing the necklace that Therodimus had given her so long ago: but it was by no means the only ornament she carried now.

"I hope the ships will be safe," she said anxiously.
"There's not much wind, and they will have ridden out much worse storms than this," Aretenon reassured her, as they entered his cave, Eris and Jeryl looked round with eager interest to see what new wonders the Phileni had made during their abscence: but if there were any they had, as usual, been hidden away until Aretenon was ready to show them. He was still rather childishly fond of such little surprises and mysteries.

There was an air of absent-mindedness about the meeting that would have puzzled an onlooker ignorant of its cause. As Eris talked of all the changes in the outer world, of the sucess of the new Phileni settlements, and of the steady growth of agriculture among his people, Aretenon listened with only half his mind. His thoughts, and those of his friends, were far out at sea, meeting the on-coming ships which might be bringing the greatest news their world had ever received.

AS ERIS finished his report, Aretenon rose to his feet and began to move restlessly around the chamber.

"You have done better than we dared to hope at the beginning. At least there has been no war for a generation, and our food supply is ahead of the population for the first time in history—thanks to our new agricultural techniques."

Aretenon glanced at the furnishings of his chamber, recalling with an effort the fact that in his own youth almost everything he saw would have appeared impossible or even meaningless to him. Not even the simplest of tools had existed then, at least in the knowledge of his people. Now there were ships and bridges and houses—and these were only the beginning.

"I am well satisfied," he said. "We have, as we planned, diverted the whole stream of our culture, turning it away from the dangers that lay ahead. The powers that made the Madness possible will soon be forgotten: only a handful of us still know of them, and we will take our secrets with us. Perhaps when our decendants rediscover them, they will be wise enough to use them properly. But we have uncovered so many new wonders that it may be a thousand generations before we turn again to look into our own minds and to tamper with the forces locked within them."

The mouth of the cave was illuminated by a sudden flash of lightning. The storm was coming nearer, though it was still some miles away.

"While we're waiting for the ships," said Aretenon rather abruptly, "come into the next cave and see some of the new things we have to show you since your last visit."

It was a strange collection. Side by side on the same bench were tools and inventions which in other cultures had been separated by thousands of years of time. The Stone-Age was past: bronze and iron had come, and already the first crude scientific instruments had been built for experiments that were driving back the frontiers of the unknown. A primitive retort spoke of the beginnings of chemistry, and by its side were the first lenses that the world had seen—waiting to reveal the unsuspected universes of the infinitely small and the infinitely great.

The storm was upon them as Aretenon's description of these new wonders drew to its close.

"I've shown you everything of importance," he said, "but here's something that may amuse you while we're waiting. As I said, we've sent expeditions everywhere to collect and classify all the rocks they can, in the hope of finding useful minerals. One of them brought back this."

He extinguished the lights and the cave became completely dark.

"It will be some time before your eyes grown sensitive enough to see it," Aretenon warned. "Just look over there in that corner."

Eris strained his eyes into the darkness. At first he could see nothing: then slowly, a glimmering blue light became faintly visible. It was so vague and diffuse that he could not focus his eyes upon it, and he automatically moved forward.

"I shouldn't go too near," advised Aretenon. "It seems to be a perfectly ordinary mineral, but the Phileni who found it and carried it here got some very strange burns from handling it. Yet it's quite cold to the touch. One day we'll learn its secret: but I don't suppose it's anything at all important."

A VAST CURTAIN of sheet lightning split the sky, and for a moment the reflected glare lit up the cave, pinning weird shadows against the walls. At the same moment one of the Phileni staggered into the entrance and called something to Aretenon in its thin, reedy voice. He gave a great shout of triumph, then his thoughts came crashing into Eris' mind.

"Land! They've found land—a whole new continent waiting for us!"

Eris felt the sense of triumph and victory well up within him like water bursting from a spring. Clear ahead now into the future lay the new, the glorious road along which their children would travel, mastering the world and all its secrets as they went. The vision of Therodimus was at last sharp and brilliant before his eyes.

He felt for the mind of Jeryl, so that she could share his joy—and found that it was closed to him. Leaning towards her in the darkness, he could sense that she was still staring into the depths of the cave, as if she had never heard the wonderful news, and could not tear her eyes away from the enigmatic glow.

Out of the night came the roar of the belated thunder as it raced across the sky. Eris felt Jeryl tremble beside him, and sent out his thoughts to comfort her. "Don't let the thunder frighten you," he said gently. "What is there to fear now?"

"I do not know," replied Jeryl. "I am frightened—but not of the thunder. Oh, Eris, it is a wonderful thing we have done, and I wish that Therodimus could be here to see it. But where will it lead in the end—this new road of ours?"

Out of the past, the words that Aretenon had once spoken had risen up to haunt her. She remembered their walk by the river, long ago, when he had talked of his hopes and had said: "Certainly nothing we can learn from Nature will ever be as great a threat as the peril we have uncovered in our own minds." Now the words seemed to mock her and to cast a shadow over the golden future: but why, she could not say.

Alone, perhaps, of all the races in the Universe, her people had reached the second cross-roads—and had never passed the first. Now they must go along the road that they had missed, and must face the challenge at its end—the challenge from which, this time, they could not escape.

In the darkness, the faint glow of dying atoms burned unwavering in the rock. It would still be burning there, scarcely dimmed, when Jeryl and Eris had been dust for centuries. It would be only a little fainter when the civilization they were building had at last unlocked its secrets.

The Star

It is three thousand light-years to the Vatican. Once I believed that space could have no power over Faith. Just as I believed that the heavens declared the glory of God's handiwork. Now I have seen that handiwork, and my faith is sorely troubled.

I stare at the crucifix that hangs on the cabin wall above the Mark VI computer, and for the first time in my life I wonder if it is no more than an empty symbol.

I have told no one yet, but the truth cannot be concealed. The data are there for anyone to read, recorded on the countless miles of magnetic tape and the thousands of photographs we are carrying back to Earth. Other scientists can interpret them as easily as I can—more easily, in all probability. I am not one who would condone that tampering with the Truth which often gave my Order a bad name in the olden days.

The crew is already sufficiently depressed, I wonder how they will take this ultimate irony. Few of them have any religious faith, yet they will not relish using this final weapon in their campaign against me—that private, good-natured but fundamentally serious war which lasted all the way from Earth. It amused them to have a Jesuit as chief astrophysicist: Dr. Chandler, for instance, could never get over it (why are medical men such notorious atheists?). Sometimes he would meet me on the observation deck, where the lights are always low so that the stars shine with undiminished glory. He would come up to me in the gloom and stand staring out of the great oval port, while the heavens crawled slowly round us as the ship turned end over end with the residual spin we had never bothered to correct.

"Well, Father," he would say at last. "It goes on forever and forever, and perhaps Something made it. But how you can believe that Something has a special interest in us and our miserable little world—that just beats me." Then the argument would start, while the stars and nebulae would swing around us in silent, endless arcs beyond the flawlessly clear plastic of the observation port.

It was, I think, the apparent incongruity of my position which . . . yes, amused . . . the crew. In vain I would point to my three papers in the Astrophysical Journal, my five in the Monthly Notices of the Royal Astronomical Society. I would remind them that our Order has long been famous for its scientific works. We may be few now, but ever since the eighteenth century we have made contributions to astronomy and geophysics out of all proportions to our numbers.

Will my report on the Phoenix Nebula end our thousand years of history? It will end, I fear, much more than that.

I do not know who gave the Nebula its name, which seems to me a very bad one. If it contains a prophecy, it is one which cannot be verified for several thousand million years. Even the word nebula is misleading: this is a far smaller object than those stupendous clouds of mist—the stuff of unborn stars—which are scattered throughout the length of the Milky Way. On the cosmic scale, indeed, the Phoenix Nebula is a tiny thing—a tenuous shell of gas surrounding a single star.

Or what is left of a star . . .

The Rubens engraving of Loyola seems to mock me as it hangs there above the spectrophotometer tracings. What would you, Father, have made of this knowledge that has come into my keeping, so far from the little world that was all the universe you knew? Would your faith have risen to the challenge, as mine has failed to do?

You gaze into the distance, Father, but I have traveled a distance beyond any that you could have imagined when you founded our Order a thousand years ago. No other survey ship has been so far from Earth: we are at the very frontiers of the explored universe. We set out to reach the Phoenix Nebula, we succeeded, and we are homeward bound with our burden of knowledge. I wish I could lift that burden from my shoulders, but I call to you in vain across the centuries and the light-years that lie between us.

On the book you are holding the words are plain to read. AD MAIOREM DEI GLORIAM[1] the message runs, but it is a message I can no longer believe. Would you still believe it, if you could see what we have found?

We knew, of course, what the Phoenix Nebula was. Every year, in our galaxy alone, more than a hundred stars explode, blazing for a few hours or days with thousands of times their normal brilliance before they sink back into death and obscurity. Such are the ordinary novae—the commonplace disasters of the universe. I have recorded the spectrograms and light-curves of dozens, since I started working at the lunar observatory.

But three or four times in every thousand years occurs something beside which even a nova pales into total insignificance.

When a star becomes a supernova, it may for a little while outshine all the massed suns of the galaxy. The Chinese astronomers watched this happen in 1054 A.D.[2], not knowing what it was they saw. Five centuries later, in 1572, a supernova blazed in Cassiopeia[3] so brilliantly that it was visible in the daylight sky. There have been three more in the thousand years that have passed since then.

Our mission was to visit the remnants of such a catastrophe, to reconstruct the events that led up to it, and, if possible, to learn its cause. We came slowly in through the concentric shells of gas that had been blasted out six thousand years before, yet were expanding still. They were immensely hot, radiating still with a fierce violet light, but far too tenuous to do us any damage. When the star had exploded, its outer layers had been driven upwards with such speed that they had escaped completely from its gravitational field. Now they formed a hollow shell large enough to engulf a thousand solar systems, and at its center burned the tiny, fantastic object which the star had now become—a white dwarf, smaller than the Earth yet weighing a million times as much.

The glowing gas shells were all around us, banishing the normal night of interstellar space. We were flying into the center of a cosmic bomb that had detonated millennia ago and whose incandescent fragments were still hurtling apart. The immense scale of the explosion, and the fact that the debris already covered a volume of space many billions of miles across, robbed the scene of any visible movement. It would take decades before the unaided eye could detect any motion in these tortured wisps and eddies of gas, yet the sense of turbulent expansion was overwhelming.

We had checked our primary drive hours before, and were drifting slowly towards the fierce little star ahead. Once it had been a sun like our own, but it had squandered in a few hours the energy that should have kept it shining for a million years. Now it was a shrunken miser, hoarding its resources as if trying to make amends for its prodigal youth.

No one seriously expected to find planets. If there had been any before the explosion, they would have been boiled into puffs of vapor, and their substance lost in the greater wreckage of the star itself. But we made the automatic search, as always when approaching an unknown sun, and presently we found a single small world circling the star at an immense distance. It must have been the Pluto of this vanished solar system, orbiting on the frontiers of the night. Too far from the central sun ever to have known life, its remoteness had saved it from the fate of all its lost companions.

The passing fires had seared its rocks and burnt away the mantle of frozen gas that must have covered it in the days before the disaster. We landed, and we found the Vault.

Its builders had made sure that we should. The monolithic marker that stood above the entrance was now a fused stump, but even the first long-range photographs told us that here was the work of intelligence. A little later we detected the continent-wide pattern of radioactivity that had been buried in the rock. Even if the pylon above the Vault had been destroyed, this would have remained, an immovable and all but eternal beacon calling to the stars. Our ship fell towards this gigantic bull's-eye like an arrow into its target.

The pylon must have been a mile high when it was built, but now it looked like a candle that had melted down into a puddle of wax. It took us a week to drill through the fused rock, since we did not have the proper tools for a task like this. We were astronomers, not archaeologists, but we could improvise. Our original program was forgotten: this lonely monument, reared at such labor at the greatest possible distance from the doomed sun, could have only one meaning. A civilization which knew it was about to die had made its last bid for immortality.

It will take us generations to examine all the treasures that were placed in the Vault. They had plenty of time to prepare, for their sun must have given its first warnings many years before the final detonation. Everything that they wished to preserve, all the fruits of their genius, they brought here to this distant world in the days before the end, hoping that some other race would find them and that they would not be utterly forgotten.

If only they had had a little more time! They could travel freely enough between the planets of their own sun, but they had not yet learned to cross the interstellar gulfs, and the nearest solar system was a hundred light-years away.

Even if they had not been so disturbingly human as their sculpture shows, we could not have helped admiring them and grieving for their fate. They left thousands of visual records and the machines for projecting them, together with elaborate pictorial instructions from which it will not be difficult to learn their written language. We have examined many of these records, and brought to me for the first time in six thousand years the warmth and beauty of a civilization which in many ways must have been superior to our own. Perhaps they only showed us the best, and one can hardly blame them. But their worlds were very lovely, and their cities were built with a grace that matches anything of ours. We have watched them at work and play, and listened to their musical speech sounding across the centuries. One scene is still before my eyes—a group of children on a beach of strange blue sand, playing in the waves as children play on Earth.

And sinking into the sea, still warm and friendly and life-giving, is the sun that will soon turn traitor and obliterate all this innocent happiness.

Perhaps if we had not been so far from home and so vulnerable to loneliness, we should not have been so deeply moved. Many of us had seen the ruins of ancient civilizations on other worlds, but they had never affected us so profoundly.

This tragedy was unique. It was one thing for a race to fail and die, as nations and cultures have done on Earth. But to be destroyed so completely in the full flower of its achievement, leaving no survivors—how could that be reconciled with the mercy of God?

My colleagues have asked me that, and I have given what answers I can. Perhaps you could have done better, Father Loyola, but I have found nothing in the Eocercitia Spiritualia that helps me here. They were not an evil people: I do not know what gods they worshipped, if indeed they worshipped any. But I have looked back at them across the centuries, and have watched while the loveliness they used their last strength to preserve was brought forth again into the light of their shrunken sun.

I know the answers that my colleagues will give when they get back to Earth. They will say that the universe has no purpose and no plan, that since a hundred suns explode every year in our galaxy, at this very moment some race is dying in the depths of space. Whether that race has done good or evil during its lifetime will make no difference in the end: there is no divine justice, for there is no God.

Yet, of course, what we have seen proves nothing of the sort.

Anyone who argues thus is being swayed by emotion, not logic. God has no need to justify His actions to man. He who built the universe can destroy it when He chooses. It is arrogance—it is perilously near blasphemy—for us to say what He may or may not do.

This I could have accepted, hard though it is to look upon whole worlds and peoples thrown into the furnace. But there comes a point when even the deepest faith must falter, and now, as I look at my calculations, I know I have reached that point at last.

We could not tell, before we reached the nebula, how long ago the explosion took place. Now, from the astronomical evidence and the record in the rocks of that one surviving planet, I have been able to date it very exactly. I know in what year the light of this colossal conflagration reached Earth. I know how brilliantly the supernova whose corpse now dwindles behind our speeding ship once shone in terrestrial skies. I know how it must have blazed low in the East before sunrise, like a beacon in that Oriental dawn.

There can be no reasonable doubt: the ancient mystery is solved at last. Yet—O God, there were so many stars you could have used.

What was the need to give these people to the fire, that the symbol or their passing might shine above Bethlehem?